WISHBONE CREEK

AND

OTHER STORIES

BY

Tom Nolan

Wishbone Creek and Other Stories

Tom Nolan

ISBN 978-0-9792293-5-0

Publisher: Millrock Writers, New Paltz, NY.

All the stories in this book have been published electronically on Fictionique (www.fictionique.com) over the past two years. *Making it Right* also appeared in print in the SUNY Empire State College literary magazine, Many Waters, in 2005 with the title *Alone Together*. This anthology is the author's effort to put the stories in a form available to those without access to computers or cell phones, rare as that may be.

The individual stories have been honed by the editorial work of Lisa Phillips. I have relooked at each one and may have made a change in one or two places myself but for the most part, the quality herein is due to the sharp eye of Lisa, any typos, or other less than stellar examples of prose are due to my meddling.

This Anthology is dedicated to two very important people in my life:

Carol – My wife and first reader - who both loves my work and is not afraid to tell me what's wrong with it.

Maureen Brown – my sister, who inspired this anthology by telling me she always takes the *Millrock Writers Anthology* I edited a few years ago as her "Chemo book" when she goes for treatment.

Table of Contents

Claire

Milosh pressed the number 4 and leaned on the Yamaha electronic piano he'd braced against the freight elevator's padded wall. Slipping the invoice out of the breast pocket of his Marvin's Pianos uniform shirt, he rechecked the ship to address. At the fourth floor, the gate opened on a short hallway about twice the length of the piano. Spying the ornate D on the door directly in front of him, Milosh rolled the piano up to it and pressed the ivory button below the letter.

A shadow crossed the view port and the door opened wide.

"Finally!" the ancient woman croaked, her teeth clamped on a long amber cigarette holder housing an unlit cigarillo. From the sleeves of her flowing gold lame robe talon-like hands appeared, waving about like tiny birds looking for a perch. As Milosh pushed the piano into the foyer, they chose to land on its top. He stopped so as not to run the tiny woman down. "No, no. Come." She turned, fluttery hands motioning him into a large high-ceilinged parlor, hung with Persian tapestries and a wall mirror that played tricks with the light. She moved with surprising speed to a spot next to a maroon velvet chaise. "Here."

Milosh unstrapped the bench from the top. Placing it upright on the floor, he removed the corrugated cardboard padding. He jockeyed the piano on the dolly until one side angled toward the floor then raised the other and kicked the dolly away. He lowered the piano, eyes on the woman who pointed, shook her head, pointed again, before finally nodding and flinging herself onto the chaise. Careful not to mar the shining ebony surface, he cut away the protective packaging and stacked it on the piano dolly, lashing it tight with the shipping straps while the old woman watched. Finally, Milosh pulled the invoice and a pen from his pocket. He leaned toward her, offering the pen, pointing to the place to sign.

She shook her head. "I want to hear it first"

He straightened and shrugged. "Where is plug?"

"What?"

He pointed to the cord draped over the ebony top.

"Oh," she nodded, smiling. Flicking her right hand toward the Persian tapestry hanging behind the piano she said, "There."

Milosh put the invoice and pen on the piano, then gently lifted the hanging and located the outlet. He inserted the plug then restored the tapestry, smoothing its surface as he did. He turned the Yamaha on, pulled the bench to it then stepped back with a slight bow, his arm stretched toward the piano like a maitre d' offering a table. "No." She waved her crooked hands. "Look at these."

"It plays." He pressed the demo key and the syncopated sounds of Scott Joplin's *The Entertainer* began.

"No, no." the woman said. She rose and flicked both hands at the bench. "*You* play."

Milosh cocked his head. "*I* play?"

She nodded. "I heard you in Kiev. I was there doing Streetcar; my Blanche was the talk of the theatre!" She sighed. Eyes locked on some distant Russian stage she circled the room, one hand on her hip, the other held high. "So long ago...you were so young." She stopped near the chaise. "Will you play for me? Please?"

Milosh frowned. He saw his history in her old eyes, his career interrupted, ended, by his escape. "So long time," he said. The woman nodded. He sat and adjusted the bench. Flexing his fingers, he asked, "What play?"

"Brahms," she answered. Smiling, she settled into the chaise. "The B Minor Rhapsody." Milosh closed his eyes. From the opening F-sharp octave, his body memory guided his touch; he swayed to the pure sounds. When the final B octave faded, he opened his eyes and turned toward the woman. She was asleep. He turned the piano off and left.

"Where's the invoice?" Marvin asked.

Milosh flinched. "On piano, sorry."

"Sorry don't get us paid." Marvin pointed to the door. "Go get it. And bring it back signed."

Milosh glanced at the clock. "It is late."

"You got someplace to be? Maybe the unemployment line? Go, go."

Milosh pressed the bell at 4D.

"You're back." She waved him in. He strode to the piano and retrieved the invoice.

"Sign please."

"Play first?" Milosh shook his head. "If I sign?" Milosh nodded. She scrawled large sweeping loops on the invoice. Milosh checked that she'd signed in the right place before he pocketed it. He sat at the piano. "Debussy," the woman said, reclining on her chaise. His fingers flew through the Preludes. When he touched the final notes of Canope, he glanced at the chaise. Her breathing had stopped.

Milosh sighed and struck the opening chords of Claire de Lune.

-END-

Sharpshooter

By the time the sound of the first shot reached Robie, the round had already split his collarbone and a second bullet was on its way to Julie's left temple. The impact spun him so he didn't see the small hole appear in his wife's head, nor did he see the much larger exit wound. What he did see was the look of surprise in Julie's eyes as life left them. He passed out reaching for her.

Red, blue, green lights. "Apply pressure there ... " sirens, rocking. "Detective Robie, can you hear me?" green walls ... rocking ... bright white light. .... "We've got you detective ..." shimmery window ... buildings lit up ... " ... vitals holding ..." shadow in the window. Sunshine.

Robie drifted in and out of consciousness, trying to focus but falling back to sleep. . "Hey partner, 'bout time you woke up." Samuel Allison stood at the foot of the bed, forcing a smile. "You been down more'n two days."

Robie's head began to clear. "Julie ... ?"

Allison's smile cracked. His eyes left his partner's face and searched for a safe place to focus, finally settling on the window. He walked to it without answering.

"Sam?"

Allison's powerful body seemed to shrink into his gray suit as he turned back to his partner of twelve years. With deep sadness in his dark face, he said, "Robie ... man ... she's dead. It was quick. A round through the temple. I'm so sorry." Robie began to cry. "God, I'm sorry. I shouldn'ta told you that way. Man, don't cry." Tears appeared on Sam's own cheeks and he turned away. "Aw, man. C'mon," Allison said, finally, "I can't go to work with my eyes all red. Knock it off."

Robie stifled his sobs, focused on his friend, and tried to cope the only way he knew how. "Who did it?"

"No clue yet," Allison said, responding in kind. "Looks like the bastard shot from the roof of that old flatiron building five blocks south, about 400 yards. There's some scuff marks on the roof surface but no shell casings, nothin' else yet."

"We need to make a list of all the assholes who might want me dead."

Allison chuckled. "How about we just take the phone book and cross out the few that don't, Robe? Anyway, I already started on it. I figure we need to look for somebody who'd even attempt a shot like that. That's gotta be a small number. Jesus, I hope it's a small number. We got seven hits so far. Four are locked up. One is on the West Coast, and we haven't found the other two."

A nurse walked in, pasted on a big smile and approached Robie's bed. "How are we feeling this morning, Richard?"

"I don't know about you but I'm feelin' like shit. And only my mother and my wi..." his throat closed around the word.

"He answers to Robie," Allison offered. "Hey, man, I gotta go catch bad guys. I'll keep you posted ... we'll find him." He disappeared into the bright hallway as the chubby nurse began checking and probing. She injected something into Robie's IV and he slept.

The next few mornings Allison came by with coffee, black for Robie, milk and two sugars for himself. They chatted about open cases, a cop's version of talking about the weather, then Allison brought him up to date on the investigation. When he left, the same chubby nurse helped Robie get up and guided him on a short walk to the nurses station and back.

On day six Assistant District Attorney Linda Wilcox came through the door. "Robie. I just got back in town," she said as she entered. She stopped at the foot of his bed worrying the strap of her shoulder bag. "I didn't know if I should come," she said with some hesitation. "I'm so sorry about Julie. How're you holding up?"

"I'm okay." Memories of the brief affair they'd had four months ago tightened his gut. He'd spent every non-working moment since it ended trying to make it up to Julie, even though she never knew about it.

She pulled a chair up beside the bed and sat, putting her hand on his immobilized forearm. Tears welled in his eyes. "Oh God, I knew this was a bad idea." She started to rise but he reached across with his good hand and covered hers. "It's okay."

She settled back into the chair. "Is there anything I can do?"

"Do everything you can to convict this motherfucker when we catch him. Better yet, leave me in a room with him for ten minutes ... then kill him."

"I'll do my best," she said, patting his hand. "Do they have anything yet?" she asked, frowning.

He started to shake his head, flinching when an arrow of pain shot down his arm.

"Oh God, are you okay?"

"Only hurts when I breathe." He said, patting her hand. She turned it and clasped his gently. They'd gone from friends to lovers and now strained, he thought, to be friends again. He broke the contact.

She smiled briefly. "I have to go now." After she left, he could still feel her hand in his. Strong and broad, not like Julie's long slim fingers.

Robie left the hospital eight days later in Samuel Allison's car. "I put some calls in to a home care service. They'll have someone at your place to help out." Robie nodded.

When they pulled up to the curb in front of his apartment and got out of the car, a large Hispanic man rose from his seat on the front steps and came toward them. "Meet Sanchez," Allison said, "He'll be helpin' you out."

"Hi Sam. Mr. Robie."

"Robie's enough, Sanchez. Good to meet you."

"Robie, give him your key and let's get your stuff from the trunk." Robie pulled his keyring and shook the apartment key free, handing it to Sanchez who walked quickly up the steps.

"Sam," Robie said as they walked toward the rear of the car, "I don't know much about home care services, but I don't think they generally employ linebackers who carry a piece. What the hell's up?"

"He used to be a state cop till he lost a kidney to a bullet." Sam shrugged. "He opened a PI and protection service about five years ago. We were in the Academy together. Never know whether this asshole might want to try again."

Robie patted Sam's shoulder. "Thanks, man."

Allison hauled a duffle out of the trunk and started for the door with Robie at his heels. Near the first step, Robie stopped and stared at the sidewalk, imagining he could see a darkish spot where Julie's head lay. Allison put his hand on his arm, urging him forward.

The following Monday, Robie walked into the bullpen about nine-thirty, acknowledged greetings from the other detectives and knocked on the open door of Lieutenant Spencer's office. "Skipper, I need to work."

"I don't need a one-armed cop right now."

"Let me ride a desk, then."

"What does your doctor say?"

"That I shouldn't play tennis or wrestle. Seriously, he's recommending that I not sit home. I can't sit home, Skip. She's there," He knew he sounded whiny, but he couldn't help it. "Please, Skip."

"Okay, okay. But here's the deal. You get the okay from department medical and psych and I'll put you on desk duty. If your head's workin' up to snuff, I can use you."

"When can I see them?"

"I'll put in the call right now. Meanwhile, park your ass at your desk and stare at the wall or something."

He got into the medical and psych offices later that afternoon and was given permission to work half days for the next six weeks.

Robie spent four months at his desk before he got clearance to return to full duty. He used the time to pore through arrest records dating back to his patrol days fifteen years earlier. Each time he found a "possible" he searched all available databases for their location, most often finding them in prison. When his search turned up an active candidate, a uniformed patrol brought the individual in for questioning. Allison conducted the interrogation while Robie looked through the one-way mirror, sweat beading on his forehead. Most were immediate dead ends but there were four that both men agreed needed a closer look. Robie did the computer searches while Allison followed up each lead. From time to time Linda Wilcox appeared, always stopping by his desk to chat for a few minutes. She showed up the day he got the okay for full duty.

"Hi Linda. I'm back on the street starting Monday."

"Great news, Robie! How about I buy you dinner tonight to celebrate?"

"I dunno, I'm pretty tired."

"You have to eat don't you? We can find a nice place close to your apartment. How about it?"

"You pressuring me, counsellor?"

"Is it working?"

"Tell you what, I'll meet you at Kelly's Irish House about eight."

Robie showered and dressed in his favorite tan suit and a black t-shirt. He clipped his holstered snubnosed .38 to his belt at the small of his. Walking the three blocks to Kelly's, he inhaled the cool evening and let his mind wander. In the almost six months since Julie was shot, he had been obsessed with finding her killer, his killer. It frustrated him because he knew the trail was getting colder by the day. The two assholes they were looking at now were probably going to be dead ends. He needed a real lead, needed a break. He had begun to believe this was a pro, a contract killer. Now he was looking for anyone who had the juice to hire someone like that. He and Sam were reaching the end of the road; Allison knew it and he knew it. The dark mood had settled in his face by the time he walked through the door.

"I didn't know dinner with a friend could depress you this much," Linda said as he approached her seat at the long bar.

"Sorry. This case is makin' me nuts. I can't find a break anywhere and the longer it takes … "

"I know, I know. Let's find a table and try to enjoy the evening." She slid off the barstool and walked toward an empty corner booth. She'd changed into a dark brown silk dress that caught the attention of almost everybody in the place when she moved. A twinge of guilt stabbed him as he thought of their history. He pushed the thought away.

They settled in a booth and perused their menus. When the young waitress appeared they each ordered Irish stew and a pint of Guinness.

"Robie, You know the chances of finding the killer are getting pretty slim."

"Of course I know," he said with some irritation, "I think of it every time I mark another day off the calendar. I just can't let him get away with this. If the fucker hadn't taken that second shot I'd have put it in cold case a month ago." Robie shook his head. "Why was he so sure he missed with the first shot?"

"Maybe it was insurance. That's a hell of a long shot, and from a down angle it's even harder."

"It doesn't compute, Linda. If he wanted to make sure, he'd have waited to see where the first one hit, then taken aim while I was falling and dropped in the kill shot. They would be maybe five, six seconds apart. These rounds left the chamber within about a second, second and a half of each other. How could he have recovered, aimed and fired in that time?"

"You're going to break your glass."

Startled, he looked down and saw the white-knuckled hold he had on the pint. Relaxing his grip a little, he took a long swallow. "I told you it's making me nuts."

When their food arrived they ate without looking at each other. As Linda finished the last of her meal she said, "I'll make you a deal. You stop talking about the case tonight and I won't tell you anything about this extortionist I'm prosecuting."

"Deal."

"Let's shake on it." Linda said, reaching her hand across the table. He shook it and felt the little extra squeeze before she released him. Searching for things to talk about, they stumbled over a couple of attempts before she said, "I started redecorating my apartment."

"Me, too. Sort of. What are you doing to it?"

"You first."

He went through a room-by-room description of his plans: about paint colors for the walls, replacing some of the furniture, and completely changing the bedroom. "I can't be in there, even now. I've been sleeping in the livingroom. It's stupid, I know but I just can't."

"Do you think a complete redo will help?"

"Jesus, I hope so. I feel like such a coward."

"Not being able to sleep where you and Julie did? That makes perfect sense to me. God, I don't know what I'd be like in your situation. Can I get a tour when you finish it?"

"You're on. What are you planning for your place?" Linda related the details of the radical approach to her "space", as she put, it for the next twenty minutes.

It was almost ten by the time they finished their last Guinness. Linda, over Robie's objection, paid the bill. "My car's right outside," she said, "I can drive you home if you'd like."

Robie got up and offered his hand to help her out of the booth. "Thanks, but I like the walk." They pushed through the frosted glass doors into the cool night.

"I'm parked right over there," she said, pointing to a red Volvo S60. "I'll see you Monday. I have to come by to pick up some records." She leaned forward and kissed him on the lips, gently. "See you around, Robie."

He walked home tasting her lipstick.

Over the next few months, Robie and Sam made their presence known, catching and closing cases, working their way back up the ladder. "Back where we belong," said Allison, more than once. Robie let his mind wrap around what everyone kept telling him, that his case was going to stay unsolved for a long time. He put the files away the day after he finished the apartment. That afternoon he called Linda's office. They'd been having dinner every couple of weeks. Their conversations had been primarily progress reports on their individual remodeling efforts. Linda answered after two rings.

"Hey, the apartment's finished."

"You skunk! I still have months of work to do."

"How about dinner and a tour tomorrow night?"

"Okay. Dinner where?"

"Casa Robie, if you're into spaghetti with my own secret marinara recipe, some broccoli in a cheddar cheese sauce on the side, and a bottle of Chianti."

"Couldn't ask for more. I'll bring desert. When?"

"Eight's good. Black tie optional." He hung up.

Robie tested the spaghetti and stirred the Paul Newman's Marinara Sauce heating in the saucepan. Broccoli florets sat in a bowl on the microwave turntable, completing a six minute cycle that he hoped was right. Mrs. Rossetti at the liquor store had recommended a Chianti so he bought two bottles. He was sampling the first one when the doorbell rang. Pouring a second glass, he took both to the door and set them on the bookshelf next to it. When he opened the door, Linda stood there in a green wraparound dress, cut low, and a black bow tie. "Here," he said, laughing as he handed her the fresh glass. "Food's almost ready. Have a seat and I'll be right back."

"Can I help?"

"I've got it covered. You can find some music if you want. The CD's are on the shelf next to the TV." In a minute, he heard Lyle Lovett's *I been to Memphis* floating from the speakers. "Good choice." "Thanks," she said from the living room.

Robie drained the pasta, dumped it into a large bowl, poured the heated sauce over it and tossed it. He took it to the table and returned to the kitchen for the broccoli. He hauled the bowl to the table then plopped the half full Chianti beside it. "Soup's on."

Linda complimented him on the sauce as they ate and chatted. By the time the meal was finished, the second bottle of Chianti had been partially consumed. Robie rose to clear the table. Linda stood to help. "I've got it," he said.

"You did the cooking. Let me at least help with the cleanup." She grabbed her plate and the empty broccoli serving dish and headed for the kitchen. They scraped dishes, loaded the dishwasher and wiped the counters and the table. "Now it's time for the tour," she said.

Since they were already there, Robie started in the kitchen, detailing the work he'd done on the cabinets. He showed the living room next, then the bathroom in the hall, the guest bedroom, and finally the master bedroom and bath. "I love what you did with everything, Robie. It's really you, really shows your personality."

"That's like telling someone their baby looks like them. But, thanks. I like the result. I've never done this before. It was actually fun."

"You're wrong, I really can see your touch in it. It's definitely a man's place."

"Whatever you say. By the way, you said you were bringing dessert. Where is it?"

She smiled. "You're looking at it."

For the next five months Linda and Robie saw each other once a week, had dinner at his place or out, then spent the night making love in his bedroom.

In June, Robie and Sam Allison caught a sniper case. Four people had been shot within days of each other, each in the left knee. The shots had come from far enough away that the victims hadn't heard the sound until they were already writhing on the ground in agony. The victims were a semi-pro football cornerback, a surgeon, a bike messenger and a physical therapist..

Robie and Allison studied the bystander canvas reports from the patrol officers and their own interview notes from the victims, looking for a direction to take. "One more time." Allison said, sighing as he picked up one of the reports.

"We've been over them, what, a hundred times?" Robie countered. "We're not gonna see anything new. No, we've gotta find a link among the four vics. He hit them all within a week and it's been another week with no more shattered knees. I think our guy was settling a score. We need to find the thread that ties all them together." Robie stood and paced the wide aisle down the middle of the nearly empty squad room. "Think, Sam. Let's try to take this apart. What do these people have in common?"

"A helluva limp," Allison chuckled, "Sorry, Robie. Devil made me say it. Let's see ... the Doc and the therapist both work with folks that are hurt," he said, his face contorted with concentration. His eyes lit up and he smiled. "Hey, a good cornerback can bust people up in a game, so maybe he's the cause of an injury." Then his smile faded. "But where does the messenger fit? Where's the connection there?"

"Maybe that's just to throw us off. Look, each of the victims was hit in the left knee," Robie said. "What say we go over the doc's records and find out whose left knees he worked on?"

It took them a subpoena and two days to find links between two of the victims, eight people with knee problems requiring surgery who worked with the therapist afterward. One of the possibles jumped to the top of the list immediately. Ed Marshall was a semi-pro quarterback who'd been showing some promise of moving higher until a career-ending injury to his left knee. Allison looked up from the data sheet. "Hey, Robie, wanna bet our limping cornerback got himself a big tackle last season?"

"Let's go see him."

At the hospital, they interviewed Ray Dominic, the cornerback, verifying that he was the tackle that ended Marshall's career. "It was a clean hit on a blitz," Dominic offered. "He turned toward me just as I hit him. Christ, I heard the crack and when I rolled off him his leg was bent backwards. Made me sick, man. I went up to the hospital after the game but they were operatin' on him. I got to see him a couple days later, told him I was sorry."

"What'd he say?" Allison asked.

"Told me to fuck off."

As they left the hospital, Allison looked at his partner. "Well, Robie. We got three out of four. I say we talk with Mr. Marshall." He wasn't at home but friends told the detectives where he spent most Friday nights. They found him sitting in a corner booth at a local bar, the only one in the area that did not have a TV tuned to some sports channel.

It took seven hours of interrogation and a search warrant that turned up a .225 caliber rifle hidden in a closet, to break Ed Marshall. He admitted shooting the four because he wanted to make all the people who were responsible for ending his career learn how it felt. "But, why the messenger?" Robie asked.

"He was the guy in the ambulance that tended my knee, probably the main reason it still isn't right. He was hard to track down 'cause he was a volunteer, but I found him," he said with a touch of pride. "You know I never tried to kill any of them," he protested. "You can tell by the shots, right? Each one to the left knee," he continued with satisfaction. "Nobody died here."

They were about to send Marshall down to booking when the ballistics report on the rifle came back. The lab tech brought it up to them outside the interrogation room. Allison opened the report. "The test bullet matched the ones recovered from the victims," the tech said, "This is one sweet weapon," he added. "Custom made, no serial numbers. This thing was never on the open market. It did spend some time in water. Didn't hurt it any though. It's still the most accurate weapon I've ever fired."

"Very nice," Robie said, with more than a little impatience. "You could have called with the results. Why'd you come up?"

"Holy shit!" Allison said, handing Robie the report. "This is fuckin' weird."

When Robie saw what Allison was pointing to his heartbeat doubled, but he calmed himself. He tried to think rationally, tried to come up with a reason Marshall would want to kill him.

Marshall stood near the door, hands cuffed behind his back, waiting for a uniformed officer to escort him to a cell. Robie turned toward him. "Ed, we need to straighten out some things. First is where you were on April 14th last year." He pushed Marshall back into the room, removed the cuffs and sat him down hard.

"How the hell should I know? Who remembers where they were over a year ago?"

"Folks who have a reason to, like me. I was being shot that night and, funny thing, it was with your rifle. Now let's try that again. Where were you?"

"Christ! I don't remember. It was off season. April ... I just ... yeah, I was on a hunting trip. One of those preserves in Texas."

"You got any proof?"

"Shit. I ... wait, I paid by credit card. You can check it." Allison left the room while Robie stared at the prisoner, trying to keep calm. Allison returned in a few minutes.

"Good news and bad news, Ed old man," Allison said. "You were in Texas at a hunting preserve ..." he slammed the printout of Marshall's credit card purchases. " But not until the 20th. You gotta do better than that." Robie stepped back to the wall, arms folded, fists clenched.

"Hey! I bought that rifle on that trip. So I couldn't have used it to shoot at you."

"You bought it in Texas? Where?"

"Uh ... a little shop outside Midland, I think. Can't remember the name. I don't even think it had one. It just had some sign about hunting rifles for sale. I paid cash for it, eight hundred bucks. Guy didn't take plastic."

"How about a bill of sale?" Allison asked.

"I handed him the cash; he gave me the gun." Marshall looked at Robie. " Hey, look, I never shot at you. I never shot at anybody till those four. You can't hang that on me."

"So you bought the rifle from somewhere you don't exactly remember, didn't get a bill of sale, and you laid out a bunch of cash for it." Allison shook his head. "I don't think so."

"I want a lawyer."

"You waived that right this morning, but okay, you can call one," Robie said. "I don't even want to talk to you. I don't want you lying to me anymore." They walked him across the hall to booking and turned him over to the desk sergeant.

"Charges?"

"ADW four counts for now, "Robie answered, as he and Allison left the room. "I'm going home, Sam."

"No problem. I got the paperwork covered."

An hour later Robie called Linda and asked her to come over. She arrived fifteen minutes later, dressed in jeans and a paint splattered Texas Tech sweatshirt. "What's up?" she asked as she folded herself into a corner of the sofa. Robie sat at the other corner and took a breath.

"I think we've got Julie's killer. Ballistics matched his rifle to the slug that went through me. He's the guy that's been blowing kneecaps off his victims."

Linda's eyes widened. "Has he confessed?"

"No, not to trying to kill me. He owned up to the other stuff though. Trouble is, I can't place him anywhere and he doesn't fit any profile that I can figure out."

Linda was silent for almost a minute before she spoke. "Have you thought about a contract killer? Maybe he's a hired gun."

"Maybe, but why'd he blow that kind of career on something as dumb as revenge? He had to know we'd put things together and come after him."

"People sometimes do stupid things when they're angry. Anyway, you have enough on him to get an ADW conviction on four counts. I could probably get a second degree murder conviction based on the rifle alone, if he doesn't have a good alibi."

"He doesn't."

Linda got her convictions. Within two months, Ed Marshall was on his way to prison to begin serving 20 years to life for second degree murder. It took the jury less than two hours to reach the verdict. She and Robie celebrated at Kelly's and at his apartment. About two in the morning, Robie lay awake staring at the ceiling. He turned to Linda, slid the blankets down to uncover her breasts and kissed them. "Mmmm ... what's up, mister? Have you got designs on my body again?"

"Always." He tongued each nipple to attention. "Always. I like the sound of that. How about marrying me, counsellor?"

"I surrender, detective." She pulled his head up, kissed him hard and rolled on top of him.

Richard Robie and Melinda Wilcox married two weeks later in a civil ceremony. Samuel Allison and Helen Raines, a paralegal in Linda's office, witnessed the event. The reception convened at Kelly's Irish House in an upstairs banquet room and the couple honeymooned for a week on the island of St. Thomas. By mutual agreement, they moved into Linda's newly redecorated three bedroom townhouse at the edge of the city and put Robie's apartment up for sale.

Five weeks after their return, Robie lay awake at 3:30 AM. He rose without waking his wife and padded barefoot down the carpeted stairs toward the kitchen. In the fridge, he located the milk and poured himself a tall glass. He walked to the living room and sat in the large leather recliner, the only piece of furniture imported from his place. Switching on the table lamp, he looked around for something to read. Finding nothing within his reach, he got up and browsed Linda's well-stocked bookshelves. He bypassed history and law volumes, instead fingering several loose leaf volumes of her law school notes, grinning at the careful handwriting and the course numbers marked on the binder. "So organized," he mumbled. At the end of the row of binders sat one marked, *Home*. Pulling it from the shelf, he returned to his chair and his milk. The first page of the binder contained a news clipping that turned out to be an announcement of the birth of Melinda Jane Wilcox, to Jesse and Milicent Wilcox of Waco. Subsequent pages chronicled the growth of an active young girl, athletic and bright; A's dominated every report card, along with words like "ambitious", "charming", "articulate", "determined." Her class pictures showed a tall, gangly girl growing into a strikingly beautiful young woman. The news clippings interested him most as snapshots of her life. Her academic and athletic achievements reported in the local newspapers spoke of a girl who was a dominant figure in her school and apparently in her town.

In the middle of the book he found a newspaper page folded in quarters and pasted so that the paper would open easily to display the full page. Careful not to tear it along the delicate folds, he opened it, exposing a remarkably clear photo of Linda wearing a shooting vest and holding a rifle and a large trophy. The headline screamed: WACO GIRL OUTSHOOTS THE BIG BOYS! "Young Melinda Wilcox fired a perfect score in a match against civilian and military contestants at a thousand yards. "At this distance, most of these folks shoot less than eighty in the bull. She shot all one hundred dead on. I've never seen anything like it," exclaimed range officer Malcolm Fox. "The most amazing part was her dropping in all ten on the rapid fire round," he continued. "It just ain't human!" Miss Wilcox takes home the ..."

Robie stared at the familiar rifle pictured in his wife's hands. The book fell to the floor.

-END-

Little Fawn

The low spring sun semaphored through gaps in the dense Douglas fir forest as Eldon sped down the winding mountain road. Around a sweeping curve, a deer appeared in front his truck; too late, Eldon crushed the brake pedal under his boot. The animal flew into the brush on the right side of the road like a doll thrown by an angry child. He slammed the pickup into reverse and backed up the hill on the shoulder, stopping alongside the thicket where the deer had landed. He flicked on the emergency flashers and ran to the spot.

Hidden from the highway, the young doe lay barely breathing, her broken body twisted at a bizarre angle. She lifted her head when Eldon neared and the pain and fear in her beautiful dark eyes saddened him. He knelt by her head, slid his Barlow knife from his pocket and flicked it open. Locating the spot behind her ear, he ended her pain with a quick jab of the thin blade. He wiped the knife on the mossy ground then closed it, and her eyes. Rocking up off his knees, he examined the body, sighing when he saw that she was heavy with milk.

Eldon scanned the treeline on his way back to the idling truck, knowing the futility of his search. He climbed into the cab and rested his forehead on the wheel. He couldn't get the image of the doe's eyes out of his head. Marlena's eyes. He'd always told her she had eyes like a doe, huge round dark eyes he could sink into and lose himself. No matter how many times he pushed the memory of them out of his mind, it came back, Marlena's magnificent eyes, alive with joy, flashing with anger, soft with passion.

She didn't cry when he left, didn't yell or curse him, just turned and disappeared into the small cabin they'd built together, shutting the rough-sawn pine door behind her. The rest of the commune went about its business as if he no longer existed.

Now he sat in his idling truck. In the valley ahead, a world he'd left a lifetime ago. Just up the mountain, the commune hidden in the dense forest; here a dead doe and an orphaned fawn. Eldon turned the engine off and went back to the doe. His knife found the artery in her upper leg. Squeezing blood out of it, he spread it on his cheeks and hands. His Cherokee grandfather had told him once that to truly learn the creatures and the land one must either become the creature or the land.

"I ask your spirit to help me," he whispered. Eldon positioned the doe on his lap, shifting until he could reach her hind quarters. Satisfied, he stilled himself, quieted his mind and body, became both the deer and the earth, and waited.

Dusk had settled by the time the fawn appeared. It approached in slow measured steps, stopped every few feet, ears, eyes, and nose busy, until hunger overrode the little one's fear; head low, it made for the nearest teat.

Eldon had no idea whether it would be able to feed or if the milk would be any good. Stymied for a moment, he remained motionless. Finally, he scooped up the startled fawn. Lifting the struggling baby over the doe's body he scuttled out from under her and hurried to his truck. He stood beside it, cooing to the fawn, nuzzling it while it struggled, listening to its mewling until it quieted, exhausted, in his arms. He opened the door and slid in behind the wheel, thankful that there was little additional struggle. He started the engine and waited. The little one's breathing was rapid but regular. He placed the fawn gently on the front seat beside him. Keeping his right hand on its body, he maneuvered the truck through a u-turn and headed back up the mountain.

It was full night with a gibbous moon midway across the sky by the time Eldon reached the cabin. He knocked, then knocked again when there was no answer. As he raised his arm to knock a third time, the door opened. "His mother's dead," he said. Marlena held the fawn's head in both hands. Without a word, she took it from his arms and closed the door.

Eldon stayed at the door, hoping it would open again, that she would forgive him his anger, that she would know it was his way of throwing pain aside, pain so deep he couldn't let it out. Finally, he turned and walked back along the moonlit path. A short distance down the hill, it forked: to the left the way to the road, to the right ... he went right. At the small cemetery he dropped to his knees beside the tiny mound of earth – his stillborn son's grave. His son, who didn't even have a name. The pain surfaced then, unstoppable tears, sobs torn from his guts. He rose and staggered around the clearing. Stumbling over a small birch limb, he fell to his knees. Angrily, he grabbed the limb and threw it across the clearing, seeing it break in two when it hit the ground near his son's grave.

"Eldon?" He opened his eyes. Marlena stood over him, the young deer at her side. She knelt and touched Eldon's cheek. "Are you okay?" He nodded. She put a gentle hand on his chest. "It's beautiful." Seeing his confusion she pointed to the grave. Eldon rose on one elbow and turned his head to see. On the mound lay a length of the birch limb with the name 'Little Fawn' carved in it. Marlena stood and reached out her hand. "Come inside. Come home."

-END-

Making it Right

John sat at the small desk in the windowed corner of their living room and tapped the space bar on the computer keyboard. The screen lit up, first displaying a photo of a deserted Bahama beach then quickly populating it with the clutter of icons that meant it was ready to work. He double-clicked the icon for his email and watched the list of unread messages appear. Scrolling through it, he stopped at **News about Emile Tibodeaux** and opened the note.

Dear John – Oh God that looks so weird. You probably don't remember me. You graduated Morgan City High while I was in grade 4. You and my brother Emile were friends all through school. I know you lost touch with each other but I thought you'd want to know that he died suddenly four months ago. I'm sorry it took so long to tell you but I didn't know where you were until I saw your sister Mae in Houma. Emile left a wooden chest, a pretty thing made out of cypress, with a note on it to give it to you. It's got an old combination lock on it but there are no numbers on the lock. I hope you can open it. Let me know where you want me to send it.
      ~Best wishes, Millie Tibodeaux Landry

John leaned forward in his chair and reread the note before answering it. The frog clock on the wall ribbited five as he hit send.

A few minutes later Beatrice scuffed into the room, tying her flannel robe around her.

"Coffee's ready," he said.

"Did you get the paper?"

"Not yet." He rose.

"I'll get it," she said, walking past him to the front door.

John went to the kitchen, filled two mugs from their odd collection and returned to the living room. He placed his on the table at the north end of the long sofa and hers on a matching table at the south end. Bea returned with the morning paper and separated the sections until she found the local news, then put the rest of it between them. John picked up the front section. Their big blond cat, Spenser, strolled in and took his place: head nestled against Bea's hip, hindquarters on the rest of the news. The morning rhythm of rustling paper and raised coffee mugs was accompanied, as usual, by Spenser's snores.

Without looking up from his reading, John asked, "Do you remember Emile Tibodeaux?"

Bea hesitated then answered. "Don't think so." She opened the *Lifestyles* section to the horoscopes, but then let the paper fall onto her lap and turned to face him. With an almost human groan, Spenser shifted so his head was out from under it. "Kate was friends with a Millie Tibodeaux." John waited, watching Bea's face, watching her gaze drift decades past.

When she came back, she continued. "Wasn't he one of the boys you hung out with in high school?"

"He was Millie's big brother." John answered, focusing on the newspaper. "He was my best friend."

"Strange that I didn't know him better then; after we started dating, I mean."

"I was at Tulane by that time, remember? Emile went to LSU after graduation and we lost touch."

She shook her head. "Some best friend."

John let the paper fall to his lap and turned toward his wife. "Things change," he snapped. "People change. We started moving in different circles."

Bea, frowned. "Don't get so worked up. I just meant you didn't even contact him when we went back to Louisiana to visit. It's just strange."

He picked up the paper and opened it to page two. "Anyway, he died a couple months back." Nothing in the front section interested him so he dropped it on the coffee table and wrestled the sports pages out from under Spenser. "I'm going down there to pay my respects."

"Why don't you just send flowers?"

"Because I want to see his grave, talk to his family."

"Do you want me to go with you? I can take off a few days."

"No. I'm going to drive. I don't know how long I'll stay down there."

"Louisiana's such a long drive. Why not fly?"

"I want to drive." He stood, picked up his empty cup and headed to the kitchen.

"When are you leaving?"

"Tomorrow morning, I think." He refilled his cup. "More coffee?"

"Put it in a travel mug, I'm going to shower."

He took a long swallow then put the cup down and followed Beatrice to the bedroom. When she disappeared into their bathroom, he pulled his old American Tourister down from the closet shelf, tossed it on their bed, flipped the latches on the hard red case and threw it open. Turning to his dresser, he hauled uncounted pairs of underwear and socks out and tossed them into the bag. He followed that with half a dozen t-shirts and several pairs of shorts. Two pairs of Levi's, his New Balance sneakers, sandals and cordovan wingtips went in next, then he returned to his closet, scanning it, hands on hips.

The shower stopped. Soon Bea emerged wrapped in a green terry towel, another turbaned around her head. She eyed the open case. "They have laundries in Louisiana you know," she said, rubbing her short salt and ppper hair vigorously.

Ignoring the comment John asked, "Where's the small garment bag?"

"Top shelf in the utility room." She selected matching underwear from her top drawer. "Why?"

"I need some dress clothes," he answered on his way out the door. When he returned with the flimsy bag, Bea was staring at him.

"John, how long are you going to stay?"

"I told you I don't know," he shrugged. "Couple of weeks, maybe longer. It depends."

"On what?"

"I don't know; it just depends." Two summer suits and a couple of dress shirts and ties went into the garment bag along with a belt. He looked everything over, zipped the bag shut and latched the suitcase.

Beatrice shrugged in return and reached for her hairbrush. "I made some tuna salad last night, would you put a sandwich together for me? And a banana, and put it in one of the lunch bags."

"Sure," John said, hefting the luggage.

"I thought you were leaving tomorrow?"

"I'm just putting them in the car. In case I change my mind."

He ferried the bags to his white Camry, opened the trunk and swung the bags in. Spenser padded through his cat door, chirping a greeting as he stepped into his litter box. "Back at ya, Spense," John said.

When he reentered the house he found Beatrice in the kitchen making her sandwich.

"I was going to do that."

"It's okay."

"I'll get the banana." He reached into the hanging fruit basket and snapped off a medium yellow one. From the cabinet over the coffee maker, he pulled out a travel mug and filled it, then got an insulated lunch bag from the top of the fridge and an ice pack from the freezer. He packed the lunch bag and zipped it.

Seven ribbits.

"I've got to get going," she said, grabbing the mug and the lunch bag. She gave him a tight-lipped kiss. On her way to the garage she scooped up her purse and briefcase. John followed her. "Get the door for me." He pushed the button on the wall, opening the wide garage door like a huge mouth. He went into the house and fed Spenser.

John showered and dressed. He made a peanut butter and banana sandwich and ate it on his way to the Camry. At the edge of the driveway, he pushed the button on his sun visor and waited for the door to close before pointing the car toward Louisiana.

Early afternoon of the third day, John pulled up to the Morgan City Holiday Inn and got a room. He unpacked his clothes, showered and dressed in shorts and a t-shirt and called his sister, Mae. After begging off using her guest room for his stay several times, he managed to find out that Emile's sister had married Willy Landry and lived in Bayou Vista.

He hung up and picked up the phone book. There were two Willy Landrys in Bayou Vista.

A woman answered at the first number. "Millie?"

"Yes?"

"John Mason. Emile's friend?"

"Oh yes, John. Y'all didn't have to come way down here. I'd a sent it to you. You at Mae's?"

"Holiday Inn. Mind if I come by and pick up the box?"

"It's not here. It's at Emile's. You remember where we used to live, on Federal? He took the place over when momma died in '98."

They arranged to meet at the house the following morning. He thanked her and hung up. Back in his car, sweat dampened his t-shirt as soon as he hit the driver's seat. With the air conditioner turned to maximum, he drove west on US-90 over the Atchafalaya River, past Berwick, Bayou Vista, and Patterson and over the Calumet Cut before turning off the highway. The road wound deeper into the swamp; its surface deteriorated until it was a dirt track, ending at a collapsed dock that sloped into the murky water like some bizarre slide. He stopped the car and got out.

Standing at the shoreline, he scoured his memory, trying to match the terrain to his recollection. Finally, he turned left into the undergrowth, his eyes defining a path that ceased to exist a generation ago. A hundred yards farther he reached the edge of a large pool. The three parallel gouges that Emile had made with his Barlow knife were barely visible in the tough bark of the smallest cypress. Five feet beyond, he saw the bow of the old pirogue poking through the mud that now owned it. Stepping carefully over to the old boat, John stood for a moment, then inhaled the pungent air, crouched and plunged his arm into the muddy water beside the bow. His fingers found their mark, gripped it tightly and pulled. It came up with a slurping noise like sucking in the dregs of a milkshake. Using a swamp cabbage leaf he wiped the mud from the ornately carved circle of cypress and draped it over the exposed bow of the pirogue. He hurried back to his car.

Eight-thirty the following morning John met Millie at Emile's house and retrieved the box. He belted it into the passenger's seat of the Camry and drove back to the swamp. When he reached the pirogue, the cypress ring was gone. He looked hard through the thick growth but saw no one. He waited, looked, and waited some more, sweat dripping from his forehead.

"You brin' de box?"

John spun around and faced the ancient crone standing by the pirogue. He showed it to her.

"Come here wid it, boy," she croaked. John moved slowly toward her, the box extended in front of him. She reached out and took it, her dried leather fingers brushing his hands. He shivered. She squatted on her haunches, looking like a burlap sack filled with dried sticks, and chanted softly, tracing the intricate carvings on the cypress lid with a fingertip, her eyes closed and her body rocking back and forth. The design seemed to brighten. Her old hands slid over the side of the box and fondled the lock. It dropped open. John leaned forward as she lifted the lid.

"Step back, boy." He did. "Futher, boy, or you see whut dis ole witch c'n brin' down." Several more steps backward, he stumbled over a root. He scrambled to his feet then stood, hands folded in front of him like a small child. The old woman's claws disappeared into the box and her eyes closed again. She bent her head mumbling softly then opened her eyes and looked at John. "De udder boys try open dis box. Don' you try."

"I don't want the box," he stammered. "Keep it, it's yours anyway."

"No, boy! De box mebbe mine, de burden be you'rn. You hab de box now."

"But, why? I didn't do anything. It was Emile and the others, not me."

"Ah, you dere, boy, you see it, what dem boys do. Dey gone, now. You de las'. It be you carry de box." She closed and locked it then rose and presented it to him.

"But I made it right! I took care of things. I ..."

"Ting like dis nebba made right. De ting last fo'evah. You carry dis. It be your burden now. You carry it till you die." She put the box in his arms.

"Then what?"

"Den it ovah." She turned and slipped into the undergrowth. He thought about just throwing the damn box into the black pond, but Emile and the other two had died, maybe because they tried to open the box, maybe because they tried to get rid of it; John didn't know and it scared him. Tucking it under one arm, he scrambled back to his car.

Back in his room, he placed the box on the night table and sat down hard on the bed. The faded markings on the top were, he could now see, a rendering of the pond he'd just left. He even thought he saw the partly submerged pirogue in it.

He kicked off his shoes, shed the rest of his clothes in a pile next to them and went to shower. The hot water soothed his body, calming him. He stayed under the spray several extra minutes before he dried off and pulled on fresh clothes.

The sun sat low in the sky. John crossed US-90 and walked down a narrow street that had long ago forgotten its name until he came to Railroad Avenue. Turning right, he walked toward the flashing Abita Beer sign at "Cherie's Shrimp Shack". For the next three hours he reacquainted himself with the various Abita brews, and the taste of shrimp that were feeding in the gulf that morning

The walk back to the Holiday Inn, after three wrong turns, took much longer than the walk down and he was hot, tired and sweaty when he entered his room. He didn't remember leaving the light on but let the thought drop. When he stepped farther into the room he saw Beatrice sitting on the near bed.

"What are you doing here?"

"Mae called yesterday. She said you were acting all weird on the phone. She was...well, you know how she gets. I told her I was coming down, just so she didn't call the sheriff or paramedics or something."

John tried to process the situation through the fog of seven or more bottles of beer but couldn't sort it out. "I'm gonna shower," he said. He started the shower hot and gradually turned the hot water down until he stood shivering. When he couldn't take it anymore, he toweled off and padded out of the bathroom, naked.

Beatrice was examining the cypress box that now rested beside her on the bed. "It's beautiful." She hefted the lock in her left hand, a curious frown on her face. John stood frozen in place. She closed her eyes for a few seconds then turned the dial right until it stopped then left, right, left. It fell open. "It's like the one Kate had." Her voice droned. "It works by counting clicks. It's so strange that it opened."

Before John could react, Beatrice lifted the lid. She drew out a white dress with pale blue polka dots, and a large dark bloodstain on it.

-END-

Checking Out

While pondering Food Lion's sparse population of cheeses something bumped my hip. I turned peering over my reading glasses to see a pretty woman behind the overloaded shopping cart resting against my right buttock. She wore a snug Carolina Blue T-shirt, jeans, and a pleasant smile that quashed any annoyance I might have displayed. "I'm so sorry," she said. "I should never shop hungry."

"I know what you mean," I said, nudging the cart slightly to remind her it still rested against me. "I haven't eaten since breakfast." She didn't seem to notice.

"I even missed breakfast." She wedged a tub of Land-o-Lakes Butter between two half-gallons of skimmed milk before she backed the cart away and moved on. I resumed perusing cheeses.

Five minutes later I saw her in one of the shorter checkout lines and slid in behind her. Focused on the pleasing arc of her hips under the denim jeans, I was startled when she turned and said, "Why don't you go ahead? I've got a ton here."

"No, thanks. I've been driving for several hours. I'd like to stand a while."

She shrugged then transferred a rump roast from her cart to the conveyor. "Where did you come from?" she asked as she reached for the two skimmed milk containers.

"Baltimore, visiting grandchildren." I admired the economy of motion in her attractive, solid body, the way she sorted her purchases as she emptied her cart.

"Do you live on the Outer Banks?" she said without looking up from her work.

"No, I have a writing workshop in Rodanthe. I'm cooking dinner tonight," I added.

"Do you like to cook?" she asked, eyes on the register while the young clerk scanned her items, and a bagger filled many plastic bags.

"I do."

The conveyor stopped. The clerk flicked the switch that set the lane number light flashing. "I gotta get a price check on the frozen chard," he said. Sighing, the woman retrieved the rump roast from the belt and explained how she was going to prepare it. I smiled and nodded without listening, focused instead on the fluid grace of her long fingers as they made slicing motions across the roast.

Aware suddenly that she'd stopped speaking, I offered, "I'll be making spaghetti, with a side salad, and Chianti."

"Sounds delightful," she said, returning the roast to the conveyor.

I placed a divider on the belt and stacked my groceries behind it. The conveyor moved so the clerk could scan the last of her items, the roast.

"Two oh seven sixty-three," he said. "Do you have our MVP card?"

She pulled a wallet from the shearling jacket hung over her cart handle. Her expression changed as she pored through the compartments. "Damn! I must have left it in the kitchen." With a sheepish look she asked, "Can you keep track of the total until I come back?" Turning to me she shrugged. "Sorry about this."

"Comes from not eating breakfast."

She smiled, shaking her head. The clerk flicked the call light on again, summoning a manager who swiped her company MVP card then handed the woman an application. She shrugged, started to put her wallet away then opened it and extracted a business card. "Call me if you need an audience. I'm a good listener."

She donned the jacket and pushed the loaded cart out the door. While the clerk registered my purchases I read the card: *Value Added Realty, Jo Mazeroski, Senior Agent. 216 Sir Walter Raleigh Street, Manteo, NC.* A phone and fax number and a black and white head shot in the upper right. I slipped it into my hip pocket, snatched up my groceries and hurried out of the store.

Hoping to see her, I scanned the lot, at the same time wondering what I'd do if I did. Invite her to dinner? Ask if she was related to the great Pirates second baseman Bill Mazeroski? What? The only thing I did know was that somewhere deep in my sixty-eight year old body, the libido of my youth demanded recognition. After a second and third scan of the lot on the way to my car, I gave up and continued south to Rodanthe.

At the beach house I turned the heat up against the January chill. I dropped my gear in the hall, stowed the food and cracked a Corona, adding a small wedge of lime before stepping outside to greet the Atlantic. On my way to the rooftop deck I slipped the card from my jeans. Propped on one of the Adirondack chairs I read it again, holding it high to take advantage of the setting sun over my shoulder. I got lost in the photo for a while, then shook myself out of it. "You're a happily married man, dummy!" I growled. I shoved the card into the pocket of my down vest and watched the Atlantic waves sculpt the deserted beach. When the sun dropped behind Pamlico Sound, the north wind kicked up, driving me inside.

I shrugged out of the vest. Hauling my bag into the front bedroom, I filled the upper two drawers of the small dresser with my clothes, arranged toilet articles, prescription meds, and vitamins in the tray on top and pushed the suitcase into the empty closet.
Finally, I removed my shoes and socks, last vestiges of my mainland life. Grabbing my daypack, I made my way back to the living room and situated myself on the loveseat in the corner.

A few minutes later, Mike called to tell me they were about an hour away. I padded over to the kitchen to retrieve the sharp cheddar and baby swiss from the fridge so they would be closer to room temperature by the time the crew showed up. I arranged them on a slicing board, located a couple of acceptable knives from the odd collection in the knife block and stuck one in each of the cheeses. Finally, I arranged the board in the center of the dining table along with a box of crackers.

Back in my nest, I opened my cell phone and told it to "Call Connie." I listened to the artificial female voice try to repeat the name, said "Yes," and waited. Her cell rang several times before switching to voicemail. I informed her I had arrived, said I'd call later, signing off with "I love you." Propping my feet on the white enameled coffee table, I closed my eyes.

"Rise and shine, old man! The writers have arrived!" John's booming bass snapped me awake.

I rose to help them with their gear. "Good trip?"

"We'd have been here sooner," Mike answered, trailing the pack, "but Eric had to pee every ten minutes."

"Not everyone has a bladder the size of Rhode Island," Eric called, already in the kitchen.

I heard a cork pop. "The Chianti's for dinner," I hollered.

"Not to worry Walt; I brought a red and a white to go with our snacks." A second cork popped.

Mike tossed linens on the appropriate beds, adding a couple of towels and washcloths to each pile and set up his computer on the tiny desk near the hall. Laurie set her writing space up on the small table in the corner of the dining area before going to her room to unpack. John and Eric brought wine glasses and the two uncorked bottles to the table.

Eric shook the box of crackers. "You have no class, Walter." Smiling, I scooted to the kitchen and searched a couple of cabinets for an appropriate bowl. I emptied the box into it then returned to the kitchen to start dinner. Grinning at the beehive of activity behind me, I put a large pot of water on to boil, adding a little salt and olive oil. I joined the wine and snack fest around the table, noticing that Eric had added dried Turkish apricots and organic almonds to the fare. "What, no brie?" I asked.

"I was leaving the cheese course to you."

"Brie ... from Food Lion?" Jo's image flashed into my mind before I completed the sentence.

"Where'd you go just then?" Eric asked.

I thought about telling him, but stopped myself. "Senior moment. I was about to spout a scintillating simile...then it was gone."

"As long as it gets to the page, you're okay, old man."

When the water reached a boil I hurried to the kitchen and dumped the entire package of pasta into the pot, pushing it down with a wooden spoon until it was completely submerged.

"Al dente, please." Eric called.

"I live to serve."

After dinner Mike laid out the plan for the following day. We said our goodnights and shuffled off to bed.

In my room I recorded every detail of my interaction with Jo Mazeroski in my notebook, scribbling until my hand cramped. I put the notebook down and turned off the lamp. Lying there, hands behind my head, eyes closed, I built a young man's vision of Jo. I saw her in a Carolina Blue shirtwaist, walking barefoot on the beach, hair tousled by the Atlantic breeze, smiling at me as she approached.

A screeching gull woke me to gray dawn peaking through the blinds. The strong smell of coffee told me Eric was up. I slipped on a pair of sweatpants and a flannel shirt and padded down the hall into the kitchen to pour my first cup. Warming my hands on it, I stepped onto the deck. "You know they'll forget you as soon as you're out of food."

"Yeah, old man, but they love me now." Eric tossed the last of the crackers into the air. We watched the aerobatic dives of the squawking birds snatching loot before it hit the sand.

"Another senior moment?" Eric nodded toward my bare feet.

"It's Hatteras. Shoes are optional."

"It's also January and forty degrees."

We watched the morning light paint the cumulus clouds over the ocean until the arc of the rising sun peaked over the horizon. "I'll do eggs," I said turning to reenter the warm interior.

"I brought green peppers and onions. Want me to dice some?"

"Sounds good. We can shred some of the cheddar that's left, too."

Eric and I worked in the small kitchen while the rest of the group straggled in, poured their coffee, and settled at the table. After breakfast we retreated to our coveted nests and quiet settled on the cottage, broken only by the sound of Mike's fingers punishing his computer keyboard.

I buried myself in my rewrite until he called "time, folks!" I glanced at the kitchen clock, surprised that I'd been working six hours.

After stowing my computer I joined John and Laurie on a beach walk while Mike and Eric took a shopping list to Avon. Beyond the shelter of the beach houses the January wind blew steady and cold. I pulled my knit hat further over my ears, zipped my down vest to my neck and reached in my pockets for gloves. When my hand touched the business card I palmed it, stuffing both hands deeper into the warm pockets.

Around ten I called Connie. In the forty years we'd been married we'd chatted almost every day, communicating by phone or phone message when separated by our various business or personal trips. I told her about my progress on the rewrite, the walk on the beach, and watching the sun come up with Eric. We exchanged I love yous and good nights as we had uncounted times before and hung up.

But it felt different.

In bed I resurrected my image of Jo, now with a hint of desire in her eyes. Her eyes! What color were they? I sat up, grabbed my notebook and read everything I'd written about her. Nothing. I dug into my memory trying to see her...I could see her smiling, oval face, the long, light brown hair, but not her eyes. Irritated, I slammed the book closed and fluffed my pillow more vigorously than necessary before laying my head on it.

Hazel! I awoke, knowing the color was right. I went back to sleep with her hazel eyes smiling on me.

The last full day of the workshop we toasted my completed second draft with 'champagne' purchased from The Blue Whale Grocery and Bait Shop in Salvo. The following morning we would part, I west to Durham to pick up Connie at her sister's, the others north across the Chesapeake to New York.

Next morning, I packed the car before daylight, made coffee, and rinsed dishes while my colleagues got ready to travel. When I'd finished, I said my goodbyes, slung my daypack over one shoulder and left. Before backing out of the driveway I withdrew the card from my vest pocket and clipped it onto the sun-visor.

All the way across the causeway to Roanoke Island my gaze kept drifting to the blue-lettered white card. At the junction of the US 64/264 bypass I turned onto the business route into Manteo.

Just past the corner of Sir Walter Raleigh and Essex, a two-story cedar shake building with a large window in the center announced *Value Added Realty* in an italicized blue lettered arc with *216* on the plate glass door to the right. I parked farther up the street and walked back. Approaching the building I tried to take a deep breath in my tight chest but managed only a gasp. I turned the knob and entered.

Jo Mazeroski sat behind a small desk well back from the window. Phone to her ear she glanced at me, motioning to the chair next to her desk. I sat and tried to get a good look at her eyes through her tortoise shell glasses (I didn't remember glasses) while she talked. Finally she hung up, pivoted her chair to face me, and leaned forward extending her hand. "I'm Jo. How may I help you?"

"Uh ... you gave me your card."

"Oh, okay." There was that heart-stopping smile. "Are you interested in renting or buying?"

"Ah ... we met at Food Lion?" I tried. "Last week? You missed breakfast?"

"Oh, sure. You were doing something down on the island." She frowned. "Something about writing?"

"A writing workshop."

"Right! How was it?" The phone rang. She picked it up, raising her hand to put our conversation on hold. I took in her appearance: rose turtleneck under a pinstriped charcoal jacket with matching skirt, hair pulled back, lip gloss and nail polish complementing the turtleneck. She hung up, turning to me again.

"So, do you own the place on the island?"

"No, a friend does." I wanted to invite her for coffee. "Ah ..."

"Would you like to own one?"

"Well, no not really."

"Rent then," she said, frowning. "I can set you up for the same time every year. That way it will seem like your own."

"Ah ... I don't think so." I rose. She looked puzzled. "I ... I need to talk it over with my wife." I hurried to the door.

"Well ... okay. You said you have my card, right?" I nodded, hand on the doorknob. "So call me if you want help finding a place."

The phone rang again as I left. I strode up the street, my face flushed with embarrassment. When I climbed into my car the card mocked me from the sun visor. I yanked it down, stuffing it into my pocket, buckled the shoulder belt and started the engine. I drove to the bypass whipping myself with a sub-verbal willow switch on the way out of town. "Stupid old man," I growled, administering the killing blow to my ego.

I reached Durham a little over three hours later and parked at the end of the cul-de-sac a few yards from my sister-in-law Marcia's house. Connie waved from the porch. I hauled my daypack onto my right shoulder and walked into her arms, lifting her off her feet as we kissed. Inside I hung the pack and my vest on a wall peg, hugged Marcia, and accepted her offer of coffee. When it arrived I raised my cup. "A toast! To my finished second draft." Both sisters congratulated me.

"How about everyone else?" Connie asked.

"Mike's still on the final draft of his novel, John's writing poetry; Eric refuses to end his memoir even though we all agree he's there and god knows what Laurie's writing, she puts words together so beautifully that nobody cares."

Marcia rose. "I'm going to get dinner ready." Connie stood also.

"I've got it, Sis. You two get reacquainted."

Connie turned to me. "Let's go for a walk."

I grabbed our matching vests from the wall pegs by the front door. Outside as we ambled toward our favorite ice cream shop, Connie snuggled into the crook of my arm. I pulled her closer, sliding my hand down her slender body to the curve of her hip. Arm around me, she slipped her hand into my vest pocket.

"What's this?" She drew the card out and looked at it then up at me. "She's pretty. Do you know her?"

I was glad for the darkness. "She's just some real estate agent who wanted to sell us a beach house."

"Do you want to live on the Outer Banks?" I shrugged.

She snuggled closer. "I don't."

I stroked her waist. "Toss it then."

-END-

The Necklace

Reece read the tiny card. *This seed fell from a rare tree deep in the exotic rainforests of Africa into the waters of a swift stream. Battling weather in its perilous journey to the sea, it found the swirling Atlantic currents that eventually washed it up on the shores of the Outer Banks near the pirate village of Ocracoke. It is said that the wearer will be blessed with great luck.* He turned the bead and leather necklace in his hand studying the rough exterior of the dirt brown marble-sized centerpiece.

Chuckling, he dropped the necklace on the counter. "I gotta have this."

A young, body-pierced clerk closed the book on her lap, rose and placed it on the chair, picked up the necklace, and said in a bored monotone. "Ten eighty-two."

Reece fished a ten and a well-worn one from the side pocket of his shorts and dropped them in her hand. She gave him change and reached for a small plastic bag.

"I don't need a bag." She shrugged then pushed the necklace toward him and returned to her book.

Tearing the card from between the beads, Reece slipped it into his hip pocket and inspected the necklace again, halfway expecting to find "made in China" somewhere. With the adjusting bead at its widest point, he put the necklace over his head, tightened it until the seed nestled in the hollow of his throat then walked out to the Manteo wharf looking for Jessie.

He saw her leaning against a piling to steady the heavy Nikon F5 in her small hands. He settled on a bench a couple of dozen feet away.

Jessie fired five quick frames, moved left a few feet then fired four more. When she relaxed and let the camera dangle from her neck, he called, "Hey gorgeous! Ready to go?"

She turned and walked over to his bench, grinning. "Did you see it? A red-billed merganzer, just floating there, posing for me. I love it!"

"I hired it specially for you. Waldo's Rent a Duck, down by the bridge."

Laughing she flopped down beside him. She blew a stray lock of honey-blond hair off her face. "Think you can arrange a snowy egret about sunrise tomorrow?"

Reece shook his head. "Waldo rented his last egret yesterday. Sorry."

"What's this?" she said, reaching for his necklace. As she rolled the seed in her fingers, examining it from all sides, the leather cord tightened a little.

"It's a seed pod from some rain forest. Here." He pulled the card from his pocket, handed it to her and watched her lips move as she read.

"How do you know it's not an egg from some exotic giant spider?"

Reece shuddered.

"You ok?"

"Yeah, I ... I hate spiders."

"Sorry. It was a dumb thing to say."

"It's okay," he said, closing his hand over hers on the necklace. "You ready to head out?"

They wove through the crowd toward Reece's yellow Jeep. Jessie hopped in, pulled their shopping list out of the glove box and went over it as they drove to the Food Lion. In less than twenty minutes they gathered supplies enough for two weeks and were off to Hatteras Island.

 He could feel the seed grow warm in the hollow of his throat, feel its roughness on his skin as they drove through the Pea Island Sanctuary toward Rodanthe. By the time he pulled the Jeep under their Atlantic Avenue beach house and hauled everything up the long staircase to the main deck, the necklace felt like part of him.

Reece opened the front door then went around to all the rooms opening windows while Jessie stowed the groceries.

"Swim?" she said as she put away the last items. He nodded.

Jessie went to their closet, grabbed two towels and her suit and tossed the surfer suit to Reece. They changed and headed out the door, picking their way across the pot-holed road toward the ocean. As they reached the beach Jessie broke into a hopping run, yelping each time a foot touched the sand. Reece walked at his normal pace, watching the ocean dance in front of him.

"How did you do that?" Jessie asked when he finally reached her spot in the cool surf.

"Do what?"

"Walk across there like that."

"Firewalk," He said.

"You've never done a firewalk."

"Have now," he smiled, stroking the bead.

They swam out a few times, body surfed back, dozed on towels for awhile then walked along the endless beach until evening. Back at the house, Reece showered in the outdoor stall while Jessie opted for the master bathroom. She was busy selecting ingredients from the fridge when he came in.

"Let's stay here forever," she said.

"Mmmm."

"Was that a 'yes' mmm, or a 'no' mmm?"

Reece wrapped his arms around her and opened her short terry robe. "That was a 'you're lucious' mmm." She turned around.

"I guess supper can wait," she said, undoing his towel.

Exhausted, they lay on the living room floor in each other's arms. "Hey tiger, that was intense." Jessie said, surveying the tiny red marks on her breasts. "Have you had your shots?" Propping herself on an elbow, she leaned over him and touched the necklace.

"This looks good on you."

Eyes closed, Reece didn't answer. He dozed, the leather cord snug around his neck, the seed warm in the hollow of his throat. *He walked up the stairs toward his room, muttering about his early bedtime. At the top, a spider dropped on invisible silk, in front of his face. He screamed and began falling backward through the air …* He snapped awake and sat upright.

"Honey, you okay?"

Shaking the vision out of his head, Reece answered, "One of those falling dreams."

"I hate those."

He nodded, flushed, sweating.

"You sure you're alright?"

"I'm fine" He touched the seed absently. "Let's make supper."

In the kitchen, Reece prepared a salad while Jessie put basmati rice in the microwave and set two chicken breasts baking in the oven.

"Seems sacrilegious to be eating chicken on Hatteras," she said, laughing.

They dressed while dinner cooked then took it out to the deck with a bottle of Pinot Grigio and ate to the rhythms of wind and surf.

Reece snapped upright in bed.

"Again?" Jessie asked.

He nodded.

"Jesus, Reece. That's every night since we've been here. You're scaring me, hon."

"I'll be alright," he said, then finally told her about the spider dream.

"Oh God, that stupid comment about your necklace!"

"Don't worry about it, Jess. It'll go away soon." He got up, slipped on a pair of shorts. Quietly he made his way down the hall and through the livingroom, out the front door and to the upper deck. Climbing into Hatteras hammock, he lay back and let the wind rock him. He stroked the seed as he watched the gray dawn haze separate into sky and sea.

"Hey baby, want some breakfast?"

Reece woke to see Jessie with a tray of toast, fruit, yogurt and coffee. "What time is it?"

"Breakfast time. You've been asleep awhile. I thought you needed it."

He swung out of the hammock and sat in one of the Adirondack chairs, squinting at the late morning sunlight. Jessie put the tray on the small table and settled in the other chair, folding her legs under her.

"Hon, maybe just feeling that thing around your neck all the time is triggering the dreams. You haven't taken it off since you bought it."

"I doubt it." He rolled the seed in his fingers. "I don't even know it's there most of the time," he lied.

"Why not take it off for a day?"

"You think it's cursed or something? It's a necklace, that's all."

"I just thought ..."

"No! Drop it!"

Jessie rose, picked up her coffee and strode toward the stairs.

"Jess, I'm ..."

"... an asshole." She said, turning at the steps to face him. "You haven't been sleeping and I'm just trying to help."

He got up, rushing toward her, needing to hold her. As he neared the staircase the necklace tightened, the seed grew hot. He reached behind his head to loosen the leather cord and felt the seed begin pulsing. Struggling to find the adjusting bead as the necklace tightened, he felt a small leg touch his throat, then another. His fingers pushed between the leather and his neck. The cord tightened more, pinning them. He tried to scream, to breathe. He tugged at the necklace, flailing wildly. His left elbow caught Jessie in the temple sending her backward, hands grabbing only air. Reece heard her head hit the steps as she tumbled toward the landing.

The necklace went slack, freeing his hands.

Jessie lay at the base of the stairs, eyes open. When he started down toward her, the cord tightened again, cutting off his breath. He sat on the top step and watched the blood soak her honey-blond hair.

-END-

Wishbone Creek

Near noon, Jonas noticed a trail of smoke over a short rise to his right and turned his mules onto the rutted path leading toward it.

When he crested the hill, the stone chimney that was its source caught his eye. The craftsmanship spoke of a man skilled in building, as did the small cabin it sprang from. Jonas observed that the yard sported a well-tended garden, while a rough-sawn rail fence enclosed a corral that ended at the beginnings of a barn. It had been framed and roofed, but the sides lay open to the weather. The jersey cow inside the corral raised her head at his approach, then resumed munching from a small haystack.

As he hauled the mules to a stop, movement caught his eye, the curtain on the front window, bony crooked fingers letting it drop. He dismounted, tethered the team to the fence rail, patted both on their well-muscled necks and made for the door. Before he reached the front step it opened and a woman stepped out. Jonas stopped and doffed his sweat-stained hat, worrying the brim in both hands. In the seconds before either spoke, he took her measure. Older than his twenty-six years by a decade perhaps, shapely in her checked gingham dress with fitted bodice open at the neck, small and fair of face with striking green eyes and hair the color of burnished copper, she seemed to grow more beautiful as he stood before her.

"May I help you, sir?" she said, drying her hands on her apron.

He had no words. He just stared.

"Are you struck dumb, sir?"

He shook his head, a flush rising in his cheeks. "No Ma'am, I've stopped to ask if you might know where I can find Wishbone Creek." He clutched and un-clutched the brim of his hat. "I'm told there's work there."

"What sort of work do you do?"

"I'm a sawyer, mason, carpenter, a builder I'd say, and good at it." He gestured to the chimney and the unfinished barn, adding, "Though not, I'd wager as accomplished as your husband."

He saw the hint of a frown on her face and thought her eyes darkened to gray, but in a blink she smiled, following his gestures with her gaze. "The war took him. Gone these four years."

"Sorry, ma'am."

"You were in the war?" She gestured to the mules.

"Yes ma'am. Lieutenant in the Ohio volunteers."

"On the Union side." She nodded. "Do you have a name?"

"Jonas Price, Ma'am." He bowed slightly.

She smiled. "I am Hannah Lebeaux, Mr. Price. Now what was it you needed?"

"Work, ma'am. And I hear there's some in Wishbone Creek."

"I expect that's true, Mr. Price. The war exacted a great cost from property as well as people." The sadness that crossed her face made him want to comfort her, but he kept his distance. When her expression brightened again he felt his knees go weak under her gaze. "Perhaps, Mr. Price, you would like to assist a widow with your skills?"

"Ma'am?"

"As you can see, I've a partially completed barn. I would have it completed so that I might move old Bess there," she nodded toward the cow, "and the chickens into winter quarters that did not include my home. I have no money to pay you, but I am a fair cook." She cocked her head to the side and smiled. "I can feed you and mend your clothing. I will tend your mules."

He reassessed the barn with his craftsman's eye, estimating the time needed to accomplish the task. There were enough straight logs a few yards away to yield the necessary lumber if he milled them carefully. The job could be done before the late October chill set in. "It will be my pleasure to complete such a well-begun structure." He straightened to his full six-feet-three. "I'm called Jonas by those who know me."

"Since I now know you," she laughed, a strange cackle. "Jonas it is. You may call me Hannah. You can set up next to the barn. The pasture behind it is well fenced and has good growth for your mules. Bess will want to be there too, if you don't mind. We'll eat as the sun peaks." She turned and disappeared into the house.

Jonas pastured the mules and the cow then unloaded the wagon, setting up his sawmill with the speed of long experience. What an exquisite creature she is, he thought as he worked. He drew into his memory the way the bodice of her dress carved her form in outstanding detail. He thought her face the most beautiful he'd ever seen, but when he tried to recall the details of her features he found they would not come to him.

Two hours later he was ready for the first log. Going to the pasture he summoned his mules, harnessed Ishmael to the dragline and brought a twenty-four foot yellow pine, to the mill. Connecting Isaac's harness to the pulley system, he lifted the log onto the conveyor, wrestling it into position for the first cut. Jonas then guided the mule onto the treadmill and set him walking at a slow steady pace that started the gears in motion, spinning the large saw blade. With brute strength and judicious peavey work he had the log completely cut into working lumber by the time Hannah called him in for the noon meal.

While they ate, she remarked on the speed of his work and the absence of waste in the result. Jonas blushed at the compliment and returned the favor by admiring the tasty and sumptuous repast she had set before him. All through the meal he took notice of her features, the blue-grey eyes, the honey-blonde hair, the high cheekbones the slender nose, expressive lips.

He committed every detail to memory, yet when he returned to his millwork he could not bring the image of her face forward.

Jonas worked until the spring sun slipped behind the western hills, stopping finally when even his keen eye could no longer measure his cuts. He relieved Isaac of treadmill duty, hung both mule's harnesses on the side of the wagon to air out. He started to rub the sweaty animals down before pasturing them for the night when Hannah appeared.

"That is my job, Jonas," she said taking the brush from his hand. "It's part of our agreement." She brushed Isaac with skill, calming the restless animal with soothing words while she worked. Jonas stared at her, wondering why he had so much trouble locking the essence of such a beauty in his memory. She finished Isaac, turning her attention to Ishmael. "Perhaps you'd like to clean up also," she said without taking her eyes off the mule, "I've a tub and soap on the back porch. The water should still be sunwarmed." Jonas's attention snapped back to himself. He stepped over to the wagon, unshouldered his suspenders and pealed off his sweaty shirt, tossing it onto the pile under the wagon seat. Climbing on the wheel, spokes he retrieved a clean shirt from his living quarters and started toward the back porch.

At the evening meal, he asked if she wanted a milking stanchion in the barn and chicken coops on the side.

"I believe both are excellent additions, Jonas."

He nodded. "I thought the same, Ma'am."

"Please, Jonas. My name is Hannah."

Jonas blushed. "I find it hard to be so familiar with a ... a fine bred woman such as yourself."

She laughed that strange cackle. "Jonas, I'm not so 'fine bred' as to want to be treated like a schoolmarm." Her golden locks swept her shoulders when she shook her head. "Not fine bred at all of a fact. Do call me Hannah."

He nodded, rising from the table. "Hannah, I'd best be getting my rest now. I should have the lumber ready in two days if the weather holds, but it'll be two long days." He left the house just as the gibbous moon crested the eastern hills.

Jonas woke with the dawn. As he hopped down from wagon bed, he saw the flutter of curtains from the window over the sink. A scant minute later, Hannah appeared with a pot of coffee and several slices of warm bread on a tray. She set it on the splitting stump. "Your breakfast, Jonas."

"Thank you, Hannah." He turned an unsplit log on end and sat while she poured his coffee. She left him there and commenced her morning chores, spreading some dried corn for the chickens then lashing Bess to a fence rail and relieving her of her milk. By the time she'd finished, Jonas had both mules harnessed, had Ishmael on the treadmill and was leading Isaac to the log pile.

The end of the second day found all the lumber milled and ready. The following morning he propped his ladders on the framed building and hauled joists up for the loft. By the time Hannah announced the noon meal, he had half the joists set and pegged and was ready to eat. He climbed down, pulling his shirt off the wagon brake on his way to the washtub on the back porch.

Hannah came out the door, her hands around a large towel as he was splashing water under his arms and on his face. She furled the towel, reaching up to wrap it around his shoulders. "You are a well-muscled young man, Jonas Price, and fair of feature." She dried his back then held the towel away. "Turn, please." When he obeyed she pressed the towel against his chest. Standing tiptoe she dried his face and shoulders then worked down each arm and finally along his stomach, all the while looking at him with her crystal blue eyes.

Overcome with lust, he wrenched the towel from her hands, tossing it aside, and pulled her close, kissing her hard. Her garments seemed to fall away under his huge hands leaving her naked in front of him. Her eyes flashed as she waited for him to remove his trousers. Once naked he lifted her by her waist and she wrapped her legs around him. He stumbled off the porch then fell back on the floor with Hannah on top and entered her. She gasped then laughed and moved with him.

Hannah brought him to heights of ecstasy beyond anything he'd ever dreamed. At times his breath would not come and yet he cared not. Dying now would be a grand death. Then she moved differently kindling new fires in him. They coupled for what seemed like hours, until he could hold himself no longer and howled at his release, a howl drowned out by the terrifying scream from Hannah as she too reached climax.

She rolled off him panting, covering his eyes with her hand.

He reached to remove it. "I must look at you, Hannah."

"Keep your eyes closed, my Jonas. Savor the moment in your imagination. I will tell you when to open them." Her hand, small,l hard, kept him blind until, almost a full minute after they'd separated, she removed it.

Jonas propped himself on an elbow to better mark the vision before him. Hannah's body glistened with the sweat of their lovemaking. The high sun lit the beads of perspiration until she appeared to be covered with diamonds. Her dark hair lay like a halo around her perfect face. Her cold half-closed hazel eyes worried him and he wanted to reach out to touch her but he fell asleep.

He woke curled under the towel. The long shadows cast by the porch pillars startled him to full attention. "I've lost half a day!" he said, shaking his head as he sat, legs dangling over the porch. The door behind him opened and Hannah stepped through. "You've been toiling mightily these several days. Rest is what you needed." She stooped and placed a tray beside him, with a large bowl of a pungent soup he couldn't identify, half a loaf of bread and a jug of milk arranged on it. "You've missed the noon meal but here is your supper." When she turned to leave, Jonas grabbed her ankle, startled at how much thinner it felt than it looked.

"I'll be staying inside tonight?" he asked.

"No, Jonas, you'll not." Embarrassed, he released his hold.

"I'm sorry, I thought ..."

"Jonas," she smiled, "I too am wearied from the day. I need my rest and my bed is small." She stepped through her door and closed it.

The next morning he turned to his work immediately after breakfast with the sun barely over the horizon and toiled through Hannah's call to the noon meal, ignoring her requests for him to rest. By evening he judged that he'd almost made up the time. Hannah shooed him out of the cabin as soon as they'd eaten, rejecting his advances. "Another time, Jonas, another time."

Other times did come through the summer and into autumn. Each was like the first, sudden, intense and so exhausting he slept afterward. Even so, Jonas completed the barn with the added hen house by late-October as he'd predicted. Perhaps it was the intensity of his toil or the discomfort of his pallet on the wagon floor, but whatever the cause, he'd been working through aches in his bones that he'd never before experienced. Late morning on the last day of October, Jonas drove the final peg and climbed down from the ladder. He turned to see Hannah walking toward him, wiping her hands on her apron, her long auburn hair blowing in the stiff autumn breeze. "It's done, Hannah."

"It is a work to be proud of Jonas," she smiled. "We'll have a special dinner this evening to celebrate both this and other news I have for you."

"What news?"

"Tonight, Jonas." She stroked his cheek, turned and walked quickly back to the house. Shaking his head, Jonas sighed. After these many months she could still stop his heart with a touch.

Following a sumptuous evening meal they sat near the fire, Jonas drinking in the warmth that soothed his bones. "I am a man of great patience, Hannah but I'm bursting to know of your news."

She rose from her rocking chair and drew down a jug from the shelf next to the fireplace. She pulled the cork, sniffed it and handed it to him with a broad smile. "Is this your news?" he said, sniffing the strong whisky odor then taking a long swallow.

"No Jonas, this is the celebration." She stood in front of him as he took another drink. "You have given me a child." Jonas choked out the harsh liquid, some through his nose. She laughed and grabbed the jug from his hand before it fell.

"I ... I, we'll wed," he choked out. "I'll stay with you."

"I know you will Jonas." She handed the jug back to him. "Now drink. You've earned it in so many ways." He put both huge hands around the jug and took a massive swallow. His eyes blurred and he shook his head, trying to clear his vision. In the fading light, as he fought to remain conscious, Hannah seemed to shrink in front of him. Her soft features became angular, her skin leathery, her hair white, her eyes black as soot.

"Damnedest thing," Martin Halstead said three years later. He waited, spitting tobacco juice into the bucket on the porch of the Wishbone Creek General Store. The two men playing checkers looked up from their game. No that he had their attention he continued. "I wus down in the holler yesterday, over where that old hag lives." He rocked his chair back until it rested on two legs. The men leaned forward as a team. "Been years since I hunted there," Martin continued. "Anyways, someone finished that barn 'n give her a wagon 'n a couple big ole army mules to boot."

"Maybe she inherited from a relative," the younger man offered.

"Maybe, but that ain't the half." Martin hesitated, gauging their interest. "They's a little girl, no more'n a couple years old, runnin' all over the place. And the hag just sittin' on the porch rockin'." He shook his head. "Damnedest thing."

-END-

Cannibals

"Sit anywhere," the waitress said, handing Ethan a menu. He scanned the diner. Two flannel-shirted truckers sat at the counter. An elderly couple shared a menu in a corner booth at the far end. A woman sat in the only other occupied booth, reading. Ethan slid into that booth.

She looked up, frowning. "Excuse me? I'm sitting here."

Ethan smiled.

"Are you going to move?"

"The waitress said, 'Sit anywhere'."

"Well you can't sit here."

"But she said I could."

"But I'm ..." She slammed her book closed, stuffed it in her large handbag, slid out of the booth and shouldered the bag. "Okay, it's all yours." She looked from left to right then stood ramrod straight. "Dammit, No!" She faced Ethan. "I was here first!"

"I know," Ethan smiled, "but the waitress said I could sit anywhere."

"I don't care what she said! I'm sitting here."

"Actually you're standing." He nodded toward the counter, "And attracting quite a bit of attention."

Both truckers had pivoted on their stools to watch. She sat at the edge of the long bench. "I'm not leaving."

"I'm glad," he said. Her angry green eyes studied him. "Haven't you ever wanted to do something like this?" he continued.

"Like what?" her glare deepened. "Bother somebody in a diner?"

"Take somebody literally," he answered. "As soon as she said it, I thought it'd be kinda fun to sit in an occupied booth."

"Why mine?"

"It was closest to the door." Ethan opened his menu. "Are you staying out there?"

She slid toward the center, placing her purse next to her.

The waitress arrived with a grilled chicken breast platter, setting it in front of the woman then yanked an order pad from her apron pocket, slipped a yellow pencil from her frizzy, soot-black bun and looked at Ethan. "What'll you have, hon?"

"Blueberry pancakes and two eggs over easy – dump the eggs on the cakes – and coffee, black." She scribbled his order, took the menu and left.

"It's nearly midnight," the woman said.

Ethan nodded at the wall clock behind the counter. "Eleven-fifteen, actually."

"You ordered breakfast."

"Is that a problem?"

She opened a paper napkin on her lap. "What do you order at noon?"

"Depends. Where am I?"

"I don't know... here."

"Breakfast."

"Why?" She cut a chunk of chicken breast and forked it into her mouth.

"Diners are for breakfast," he answered, "and we're about the same age."

Her forkful of broccoli stopped mid-trip. "What?"

"Another reason I sat here." He held out his hand. "My name is Ethan." She ignored his introduction, retrieved the book from her purse and opened it.

Ethan was about to try again when the waitress slid a mug of black coffee in front of him, sloshing a little onto the table. He reached for the sugar, heaped the spoon twice then stirred the brew. She pushed her dark brown hair away from her face with the back of her hand then turned the page of her book.

"Do you know why Americans change hands when they eat?" He asked. She turned another page.

"Neither do I, but I've always been curious. Don't you ever wonder about stuff like that?"

"I'm reading," she replied without looking up.

"What are you reading?"

With a long sigh, she answered, "Martian Chronicles," eyes still on her book.

"Ray Bradbury."

She raised her head. "You know it?"

"I love Science Fiction. Heinlein's better, though."

She sat up straight, glaring. "Heinlein's a sexist!"

"He's still great."

"How can you say that?"

Ethan mouthed, "He's ... still ... great."

Her look softened. "Literal, again?" A hint of a smile appeared.

"It's kinda fun. I may never stop."

She shook her head and went back to her food and book.

He tried again. "I'm Ethan."

She looked up. "Marjory."

The waitress arrived with his meal and the two of them settled down to eat. Ethan ate quickly, finishing at the same time as Marjory. The waitress reappeared . "You folks want dessert?" she asked, gathering their dishes.

"Rice pudding," Marjory answered. "No whipped cream. And hot tea."

"Me, too. And more coffee."

The waitress raised an eyebrow. "You want tea and coffee?"

He chuckled. "Just the coffee." She scribbled and left.

Marjory frowned. "Rice pudding with breakfast?"

"Why not?"

"You're strange."

"Stranger in a Strange Land. Just call me Michael Smith."

"Valentine Michael Smith," she corrected. "And, typical of Heinlein, Smith was a cannibal."

"So you've read it."

"How else would I know he was sexist?"

"Good point."

The waitress returned with their drinks and desserts. She retrieved two checks from her apron, glanced at them and placed one at each corner of the table, face down.

"Cannibalism was a sacred ritual to Smith," Ethan argued. "A way to honor the dead."

"I'm eating." She dug into her pudding.

"Sorry." He scooped out a spoonful. "Actually, I think Heinlein had a lot of respect for women."

"How can you say that?" she asked then raised her hand like a traffic cop. "I mean, what makes you think that?"

"The women in Stranger were smart, strong, beautiful, and ..."

"... horny, great cooks, and subservient to men," she finished.

"I'll give you great cooks and horny. But how were they subservient?"

"Dropping everything when that old fart, Joshua, hollered 'Front!' for example."

"His name was Jubal, and they were his recording secretaries," Ethan said. "They worked for him."

"Naked."

"He appreciated beauty."

"Naked."

Ethan shrugged. "There any way I'm gonna convince you?"

"No," Marjory answered, scraping out the last of her pudding.

Ethan reached for her check but she slapped his hand. "No."

"When can we continue my defense of Heinlein?"

Frowning, Marjory stared at him for several seconds then fumbled in her purse. "Give me your pen."

Ethan handed her his Bic Rollerball. She wrote on the back of a business card then put it face up on the table. "My number's there." She pointed to the corner of the card. She slid out of the booth, picked up both checks and headed for the cashier.

He slid out to follow, but Marjory turned and pointed to the booth, silently ordering him back. He retrieved the card, flipped it over and read, *Maybe I'll have you for dinner.*

-END-

Sarge

I woke up on a beach, the sun threatening to melt my eyeballs if I let it in. It took a tick before I thought I knew what year it was, another before I was actually sure of it, and another before I focused on the naked woman beside me. Her face was partially covered by long, sun-bleached hair. Her body, tobacco brown except for the pale image of a string bikini, wasn't immediately familiar, but I thought that would come when I'd completely regained consciousness. I resisted the urge to examine her person for clues. I supposed, based on our mutual nakedness, that some examination had already taken place; I sincerely hoped it had.

The rise and fall of her breasts mesmerized me for more than a minute, then several realizations thrust themselves into my brain like shards of glass: I had no clue who she was, I didn't know what beach we were lying on and I didn't know where we met or what we did last night, or perhaps for the last couple of nights, since I also had no idea what day it was. The first memory that was able to clear the haze had me walking into Paulie's about six on Friday, high-fiving Artie and Mac then settling onto a barstool to drink myself stupid and watch whatever ballgame happened to be on the nearest TV.

I shook my head to clear it - bad idea; the remains of my brain banged against my skull in an effort to escape the alcoholic hammer. When I groaned, her breathing changed rhythm; her eyes opened, closed, opened wider. They were emerald green. She frowned then smiled exposing white teeth with a tiny chip in the corner of the right incisor.

"Hi, Sarge." She stretched catlike from the tips of her fingers to the tips of her toes.

"Hi yourself," I managed.

"Did you behave last night?" she asked, raking her fingers through her hair while I watched her body sink back onto the sand.

"I hope not." I tried unsuccessfully to duplicate her stretch, and ended up groaning again instead.

She chuckled. "Having a little trouble old man?"

"Having a lot of trouble."

One of my brain cells fired, triggering a dim memory of her sitting alone at a corner table. She had worn a flowered halter-top mini-dress and a come-hither smile. I remembered now, I had downed my fourth scotch and gone hither.

"Poor baby," she said, patting my shoulder. "Question?"

"Long as it's a quiet one."

"I'll whisper." She rose on one elbow, leaning close. "Last night, when I asked your name you said 'Call me Sarge.' Do you have another name?"

"Harlan Richards." Her body felt warm against me.

"Why 'Sarge'?"

"Thirty-four years in the Air Force."

I wanted desperately to remember this woman's name. Even my addled brain recognized something special in her, a feeling I hadn't had about anyone, man or woman, in way too long.

Remember, remember –

"Are you all right?" she asked, concern in her voice.

I nodded, hoping for a hint. Finally I gave up. Opening my eyes, I sighed and turned my head to look into her face. "I have a confession."

"You're married."

"No, I---"

"You're terminally ill."

"No ..."

"You don't like me."

I put my hand over her mouth. "No ... I mean, I do like you. Let me finish, please?" She nodded. I went for sheepish. "I can't remember your name."

She laughed. I felt my face redden. She took pity on me. Choking her laughter off with some difficulty, she kissed my cheek. "I never told you my name."

"You didn't?" She shook her head, biting her lip. "Why not?"

"You never asked. You were very drunk, and it was pretty clear you wanted to jump my bones. Since I also wanted to jump yours, it seemed like extraneous information." She touched my cheek. "You looked so pitiful just now."

"I think I popped a vein," I said. "What *is* your name?"

Smiling, she answered. "Cassandra Sloan. Cassie for short, not Sandy. Call me Sandy and I'm gone."

"Okay, Cassie. Want to get some breakfast?"

We found our clothes on the sand near the passenger's seat of my Jeep, shook the beach out of them, and dressed. Cassie did some magic with her hair, using her fingers for a comb then giving it a couple of twists. Suddenly, I saw her again the way she looked last night (another memory cell was working) and congratulated myself on my excellent taste. Not to mention luck.

"Maybe later, Sarge," she said, reading my mind.

We got our bearings and climbed into the Jeep, heading north into Avon. We ate at a small Jamaican café on the Sound side. The place looked very much like it was once a rental unit, eight feet off the ground on its pilings, with evidence of several bedroom walls being knocked out to form a marginal dining room.

The kitchen had been expanded into the old dining area and enclosed with a pass-through shelf.

"Sit where you like," came a voice from behind the kitchen door.

"How about on the deck?" I asked.

"Where you like." The owner of the voice, a squat, sturdy woman about my age, emerged from the kitchen with a menu. She handed it to us and returned to the kitchen without guiding us to a table. Cassie and I were standing in the middle of the room browsing the menu when the woman returned with a pad and pencil.

I picked something called a *Jamaican Jerk Omelet*; Cassie ordered the same. We added black coffee to the order before returning the menu. "We'll be on the deck," I said.

"Where you like," the woman said on her way back to the kitchen.

Surprisingly soon, the food arrived at our table on the deck; the spicy omelet pushed me about eighty percent toward feeling human again, and Cassie's laughter made me glad I was.

Breakfast done, we climbed back into the Jeep. "Where to?" I asked.

Cassie laughed; just a hint of sun-induced crows-feet showed around her eyes. "Bet you're hoping for 'where you like'."

"It crossed my mind."

"Not today, Sarge. This gal needs some sleep."

"We could ..."

"Alone." She patted my leg. "There'll be another time. Promise." She clipped the seat belt closed. "Take me home."

Home was an apartment over a novelty shop in Salvo. She wrote her phone number in the dirt on my dash before planting a quick peck on my cheek. She leaped out before I could grab her for a real kiss.

I drove the few miles to Rodanthe and the old diesel bus I'd converted into a home. It rested on a lot right on the shore of Pamlico Sound, one I'd bought after my second promotion. A copse of scrub oaks and southern red cedar served to both hide it from the road and subdue the endless traffic noise in the summer. I'd paid eighteen thousand for it at the time---it was almost an acre and I turned down offers in the high six figures on a regular basis.

My seven-year old black lab, Rocco, crawled out from under the bus growling. "Yeah, I know, Roc. I'll get you some food." I fed him and showered in the outside rig near the edge of the trees. Hauling an old quilt out of a storage compartment that once held the luggage of bygone Trailways riders, I spread it in the shade and stretched out to air dry.

By the time Rocco nudged me awake, the sun had invaded my space, inviting perspiration to join it. It was noon. I showered again and dressed in my work clothes: shorts, a gray *Soundside Sandwich* T-shirt, and sandals.

I pulled into my slot at *Soundside* just as the digital clock on my dash flashed one. My foot caught the edge of the doorsill as I hopped out, landing me on hands and knees.

I looked up to see the huge black form of Roosevelt Marcus Jackson, *Soundside Sandwich*'s owner, standing over me.

"Begging won't do a damn bit of good, Sarge – although from what Mac tells me, it worked for you with some sweet thang at Paulie's last night."

I made a mental note to kill Mac.

"I'd fire your skinny white ass, 'cept your the best cook I got." He turned and hauled himself into his Cadillac Escalade. He rolled the window down. "Gotta pick something up in Manteo." Gesturing over his shoulder with his kielbasa-sized left thumb, he added "Rita's handling everything right now, so you get your butt over there 'fore she knifes one of those young surfer boys hittin' on her." I did as directed, saving any smart repartee for a time when Rosie was in a better mood.

Rita had more ink on her slender body than Tolstoy's *War and Peace*. There was no area of unadorned skin visible around the edges of her black tank-top and shorts. I suspected there was none anywhere else. Her short hair, dyed a deep maroon, fit her head like one of those feathered bathing caps old ladies sometimes wear. When she saw me, she growled pretty much like Rocco, causing her nose-ring to do a funny little dance. She flipped the lone burger on the grill, tossing the spatula at me afterward in a single fluid motion. "You're late, motherfucker." She stepped away from the grill, turning her attention to the two young men at the counter.

"I love you too, Doll," I said. She didn't worry me when she was pissed.

Rosie rolled in around six, pushing through the door with a keg in each hand. "New micro-brew from Elizabethtown. Catch the fridge for me." I opened the door to the walk-in, stepping aside to let him through. He lifted both kegs onto the nearest empty shelf as if they were five-pound dumbbells, instead of hundred and sixty pound buckets of beer. "We'll let them cool a couple of days." From the fridge he went to the register, smiling as he counted several hundred dollars out, leaving just enough to make change for the hour-and-a-half left in our day. "Not bad." Scanning the Sound and the lawn between *Soundside* and the shore, he nodded. "You two take ten. I'll handle things until the seven o'clock crowd starts."

Rita went to her normal roost, on the wall bordering the deck. She lit up as soon as she was settled. Having no particular place to 'take ten' I followed her, parking my carcass on the wall a few feet away. "That stuff's gonna kill you," I said by way of conversation.

Turning very slowly, she squinted at me, cocking her head. She stayed that way, not speaking, not moving, cigarette growing a long ash between the fingers of her left hand, until I finally said, "What?"

"You don't look like my mother."

"What's that supposed to mean?"

"Why do you give a fuck whether I live or die?"

Flummoxed, I stammered, "Well... because I like you."

"Bullshit."

"Really." This wasn't the way I was expecting our dialogue to go. "You're like a daughter to me," I tried.

"Granddaughter, you mean."

"I'm not all that old."

"Bullshit."

"That your answer to everything?"

"Only to bullshit."

"I'm only fifty-four. What are you? Twenty-two, Twenty-three?"

"Seventeen."

"Bullshit!" She shook her head. "Does Rosie know?"

"Know what?"

"How old you are, smartass." She shrugged. "Tell him," I ordered.

"Fuck you. Why do you care?"

I didn't know how to answer that. I had no idea how North Carolina felt about minors serving booze or any of that crap. What I did know was I cared about Rosie and for that matter, the tattooed twit next to me. They were part of my world, and I liked my world. I stared hard at her. She stared hard back. I took a deep breath and gave her my answer. "Because I care what happens to the big oaf. He's good people and deserves respect. You're going to give it to him or I swear on your tattoos, I will take you over my knee and wail hell out of you."

"Bet you'd like that."

"Trust me kiddo, *you* wouldn't." I swung around and planted my feet on the deck.

"Let's go back to work."

We replaced Rosie behind the counter just as the sunset watchers started to assemble and order their dinner. Rita kept glancing over from time to time to see what I was doing.

Maybe I actually got through.

She left a few minutes before closing, heading for Rosie's office. I patted myself on the back. I whistled while I cleaned the grill and wiped everything down.

I had just turned the key in the lock when a huge hand locked on my shoulder, turning me around to face an angry Rosie. "Puppy, what the fuck happened?"

"What do you mean?"

"Rita quit."

"What?"

"She walked into my office, said, 'fuck it, I quit!' and left." His grip tightened. "What happened?"

"Rosie, ease up. I can't talk and scream in pain at the same time." He let go and retreated half-a-step, waiting. "Look man, we were talking on our break and it came up that she was only seventeen. I told her she needed to tell you. That's it, man. I swear."

"Shit." He slammed his hand against the wall sending a shudder through the building.

"What kinda businessman you think I am? I had her social security number, her prior address, references, all that shit. I checked her out. I have a PI buddy up in Raleigh who dug deeper. You know – the ink and hair and Goth crap. Rita's cool."

"Then why'd she quit?" Absorbing Rosie's thoroughness, I wondered what he might know about me. Probably more than I wanted him to.

"That's what I'm asking you." He leaned against the wall, arms folded.

I related our conversation in detail. When I came to the part about spanking her he shook his head, a wry grin on his face.

"There it is. Her old man smacked her and her mother around. Did more than that to the girl by promising not to spank her. Fucked her up pretty bad."

I felt like crap. "I didn't know, Rosie."

"'Course you didn't. That's gotta be it though."

I had to agree, then a thought struck me. "How did *you* know? Did she ...?"

"Hell no. My buddy. Former cop, turned DA, retired to be a private eye. Man's got a lot of friends in a lot of places."

I had to ask. "You run a similar check on me?"

"You work for me, don't you?" I took that as a 'yes.' "Puppy. You need to get Rita back here."

"How ...?"

"You'll figure it out." He turned away heading for the parking lot. I caught up with him.

"Where's she staying?"

"She's crashing with a bunch of the summer kids at one of Reena's places, over by the KOA." He stopped and turned. "I know this wasn't your fault, not totally, but – and listen carefully to what I'm tellin' you – I want that girl where she'll be safe. That means where I can keep an eye on her." He dropped both hands heavily on my shoulders. "Don't let me down, Puppy."

I didn't know how, but I knew I was going to try my damnedest to bring Rita back to *Soundside*. Cassie's number was still visible in the dash dirt. I grabbed my cell phone and called it.

"Hello?"

"Cassie? It's Sarge."

"Hi. You sound a little weird. Unless that's the way you sound alert and sober; I haven't got a reference point you know."

"Funny." I had no idea why I wanted to get her involved. Yes I did. I had told this little girl I was old enough to be her father then that I'd spank her if she didn't behave. I didn't have a clue how to fix it. "I need your help."

"What about?" All the humor was gone from her voice.

I explained the whole thing start to finish, ending with Rosie's veiled warning. When I'd put a period on the last sentence there was silence. "Cassie? You still there? What do you think?"

"Where is she staying?" I told her. "Pick me up in ten minutes."

She was waiting in front of the novelty shop when I arrived. She hopped in and buckled up then said, "Go." When we neared house she said "Stop here and wait."

"We're a hundred yards away."

"Just stay here."

"Shouldn't I go in with you?" She stared at me like I was the village idiot for a second or two, then hopped out and walked quickly toward Rita's place. I couldn't help admiring the swing of her hips under her shorts, how the curve of them connected with that strong back, how .... I mentally dope-slapped myself. This was serious shit. I had to keep my mind on business. So I watched without thinking about jumping her bones ... mostly.

Cassie climbed the staircase to the deck. I lost sight of her when she turned the corner to the front door. I wanted to start the engine and creep a few feet closer but it was pretty clear, even to my woman-ignorant brain, that Cassie wanted me out of sight. I waited, and waited, and waited. After the longest half-hour I have ever experienced, Cassie re-appeared on the deck- alone. "Aw, shit." I started the engine and rolled along the shoulder to meet her.

She hopped in and buckled up. "She'll be at work tomorrow."

"How did you ...?"

"I told her you were an ignorant old asshole, but harmless, and that if you hassled her anymore Rosie would snap you in two."

I frowned, not sure how serious she was. "And that took half-an-hour?"

"No, that took about five minutes." She turned in her seat to face me. "The rest of the time we compared notes about you."

"What notes?" She just laughed. "You better tell me or I'll take *you* over my knee."

"Rosie's a friend of mine, too." She leaned over and kissed me. "Drive me to your place."

Rocco greeted us with his half-hearted watchdog bark as we drove up to the bus. "That's Rocco. He's not good with strangers," I said as Cassie got out. "Be careful."

She dropped to her knees, arms outstretched. "Hello Rocco, come here sweet boy." I watched my property guardian melt into her embrace like a puppy then roll onto his back for a belly rub. I made a mental note to talk to him about watch-dogging.

"I'm going to shower the *Soundside* off." I pointed to the outdoor stall. "Want to join me?" She glanced briefly at the stall, at me, at Roc, then nodded, rising in one of those yoga moves that made my creaky old bones envious. I stepped out of the sandals, dropped trou, and left my T-shirt as the last breadcrumb on the trail to the stall.

The water was warm by the time Cassie stepped through the plywood door. Holding it open she called "C'mon sweetie." Rocco accepted her invite enthusiastically, and I wound up pinned in a corner of the stall while she soaped the ecstatic mutt, rinsed him, then shooed him out. "He needed that," she said, facing me. "You don't smell so good either."

The luxury of being bathed by a beautiful naked woman is second only to bathing said naked woman. I couldn't wait for the dry cycle.

When we were clean I hustled us to the bus ahead of the mosquito armies, grabbing handfuls of clothes on the way. I ordered Rocco to stay outside. He growled. Cassie kissed him on the head, assuring him it would be alright. He wagged his tail. Even with her ill-advised stop to console the cur, we made it inside unbitten.

We adjourned to the bedroom and got all sweaty. Later, while Cassie dozed, I nuked a couple of yams, whipped up a salad with some greens, dried cranberries, and hardboiled eggs. We ate in bed, washing the food down with Killian's Irish Red. We got sweaty again.

I woke at five-thirty the next morning to the smell of bacon and the sound of "Sweet Home Alabama"

coming from the kitchen. Slipping on the nearest pair of shorts, I padded down the hall.

"'Morning sleepyhead," She said without turning.

"The sun isn't up yet." My Air Force sweatshirt never looked better. "What are you doing?"

"Cooking breakfast. Want some?" I wrapped my arms around her from behind. "I meant breakfast."

"That, too," I said, turning her around. Rocco growled. "Hey! Remember who feeds you, Roc." He growled again.

"It's okay, sweetie." The big goofball's tail beat the floor at the sound of her voice.

"So you've stolen my dog. What else?"

"We'll have to wait and see. Let me go so I can feed you."

"This is great!" I said, swallowing the first mouthful of egg. "You from Alabama?"

"Was that some kind of segue?"

"I heard you singing." She nodded. I found out between bites of omelet that she lived in Clanton, Alabama, was born and raised in San Diego, went to college at USC, and was a school psychologist in Montgomery. "That helps me figure out how you connected with Rita."

"You told me all I needed. She's a scared little girl trying to make it in a world of big scary men. Anyone over forty triggers 'Daddy' in her mind."

"So what do I do?"

"What do you mean?"

I picked up our empty plates. "We work together every day at close quarters in that sandwich bar. I can't unsay the crap that happened yesterday." I retrieved the green washbasin from under the sink. "Do I just apologize and let it go?" I filled it with hot water and added dish soap.

"Yes. Make it simple, not whiny. And don't engage in any verbal jousting when she tells you to go fuck yourself." She came up beside me. "Where are your dish towels?" I pointed a soapy finger at the top right drawer of an old dresser next to the kitchen table.

"Will she accept the apology?"

Cassie shrugged. "In her own way I think she will." She chuckled. "She knows something about you that ordinary people on Hatteras don't."

I handed her the last dish. "What?"

"That you have a cute little dimple on your left butt cheek."

It was my turn to laugh. "Darlin', that's no dimple, it's a bullet hole." She turned pale. I caught the plate just as it left her hand. "Hey! It's an old wound, very old.

No worries." I put the plate on the table and held her while she steadied herself. "Cassie! What's wrong?"

She took a couple of deep breaths, bringing color back to her cheeks, before she answered. "Whoa! I don't know. It just all of a sudden hit me. I have no idea why I reacted like that." She eased into the nearest chair, taking a few more long breaths. I knelt in front of her. "What did you do in the Air Force anyway?" she asked.

"I was in for thirty-four years. Lots of things - in lots of places." I knew she wanted more. "I was a little slow on my feet diving for cover."

"Where? ... When? ... Why? ... Who?"

"You sound like a reporter." I held her hands. Rocco growled. "Shut up, Roc." I locked eyes with her, waiting until I had her full attention. "The 'where' is somewhere I shouldn't have been; the 'when' is twenty-three years ago, February; the 'who' is obviously the folks who didn't want me there; the 'why' I'll tell you someday when we're an old married couple sitting in our porch rockers." I stood, pulling her with me, and wrapped her in my arms. "Your turn. Why the reaction?"

She pushed against me, shaking her head. "Take me home, please."

The ride to the novelty shop was eerie. I tried twice to start a conversation. Nothing. She walked to her door without turning. "I'll call you later," I said to her retreating back.

And she was gone. I had four hours before I would be flipping burgers. Four hours that in another life, a pre-Cassie life, would have been easy to fill. Now I didn't know how.

When I drove up to the bus, Rocco crawled out from his cave under the rear axle. He cocked his head. "Beats hell out of me, Roc." I fed him then pulled one of the white resin chairs away from the matching table and sat. My profound ignorance of the other fifty-one percent of the human population had reached epic proportions. In less than twenty-four hours I'd scared the crap out of a troubled girl and alienated a woman that I didn't really know but was pretty sure I loved. "Nice going, Sarge." Rocco loped over and sat, resting his head on my leg.

As directed, I apologized to Rita who, as predicted, told me to go fuck myself. However, our teamwork was back without any sidelong glances or subtle avoidances. When she took a break I let her alone. When we closed for the night, I walked to the parking lot with her. I said, "Good night" as I climbed into my Jeep. She grunted and walked on. That was pretty much our routine for the next four days.

Then on Saturday two testosterone heavy twenty-somethings couldn't take a hint. They kept hitting on Rita; she kept blowing them off – none too gently. Until, as she set two more beers on the counter for them, one grabbed each wrist, and they tried to haul her over the counter. Her screams made me turn from the grill. I dropped the spatula and reached her in two steps and grabbed her waist to keep her from going over. While I was trying to figure out how to keep hold of her and stop them, Rosie appeared with the speed that made him a ten-time all-pro on the Chicago Bears defensive line. He clamped a huge hand on the shoulder of each young stud, precisely the shoulder that was attached to the arm that was attached to the hand yanking on Rita. Both hands opened, accompanied by cries of pain. She and I fell backward, landing hard against the door of the fridge. I release her and regained my balance. We both watched Rosie.

"Ow! Jesus that hurts!" From the one who's right shoulder was clamped.

"Fuck man, Your hurtin' me." From Mr. Left Shoulder.

Rosie smiled. "I ain't even begun to hurt you." Lifting both transgressors off their feet like rag dolls, he backed away from the counter. "Close the shop."

"We'll be getting the sunset rush soon," I said

"Just until you get things cleaned up." He hauled them, howling toward the parking lot. "And call 911, Puppy. Seems like a couple of surfers had an altercation in our lot."

I reached for the phone beside the fridge door. Grabbing a damp rag from the sink and the spray bottle of cleaner, Rita wiped the spilt beer from the counter then pushed the button that brought down the metal curtain.

She turned, facing me. "Thanks, I mean ... you didn't have to." I nodded, completed the 911 call, and went to work. I tossed the overcooked burgers and chicken then started scraping the grill while Rita straightened things up around the counter.

"Sarge?"

"Uh huh."

"You break up with Cassie...?"

I stopped scraping. Several responses, from smartass to maudlin, jumped into my head. "Why do you ask?" came out.

She shrugged, continuing to arrange cups and condiments, her back to me. Finally, she said. "We been havin' coffee last couple of mornings." More arranging and straightening then, "She looks sad when we talk about you."

That stopped me cold.

"I ..." I stopped before I got myself in more trouble. "What do you or she say about me?" I raised my hands defensively. "Just curious."

"Well, she asks me how things are going here 'n I tell her ..."

"Tell her what?"

She stopped arranging and turned to look at me. I saw a glint of mischief in her eye.

"That you're still a motherfucker, but you ain't so bad." She turned away.

My brain got ahead of my mouth for once, informing me that this abused child had just made a remark to a father-figure with whom she was alone in a small locked area, and she did it with no fear and enough trust to turn her back. "I take that as high praise, thanks."

"You didn't answer my question."

I sighed. "I think she broke up with me."

Rita rinsed the towel in the sink and hung it to dry then leaned against the counter. "How'd you fuck up?"

For no reason other than the need to share my crap with somebody other than Rocco, I laid out the story of Cassie's reaction to the bullet hole in my butt. "I have no clue what triggered it. It's not like I go around shooting or getting shot at." I shook my head. "Christ, Rita, I'll never understand what goes on in a woman's mind."

She laughed then, a shy small laugh. "Fuckin' a."

We reopened in time to satisfy the cravings of the sunset crowd, adding another several hundred to Rosie's coffers. As I climbed into the Jeep after closing, Rita waved and hollered "See ya tomorrow." And the world didn't end.

My weekend is Monday and Tuesday, routinely slow days at *Soundside* when Rosie handled the shop with Mac cooking. I woke at six feeling the warmth of a body against my back; when my brain cleared I realized it was Rocco. "Out!" I pushed him with my butt. Groaning like an old man, he slid off the bed. I listened to the tick-tick of his claws on the tile then the squeak of the springs on the daybed that served as my living room sofa. I got up with a similar groan, padded into the kitchen to push the button on my coffeemaker, grumbling when I saw it wasn't primed. I stared at the coffeemaker then at the half-pound of Kona leaning against the blender then back at the machine. "Fuck it."

I had two days to kill, not usually a problem - not usually. I thought about paddling my kayak up to Pea Island; I thought about riding my bike to Ocracoke; I thought about building a garage for the Jeep; I thought about a dozen other improbable projects, but instead I sat outside in a resin chair, nursing a beer, with Jimmy Buffet blaring through the open windows. Rocco slept beside me, his snout resting on my bare foot.

I launched my second empty toward the bin beside the front door, bouncing it off the aluminum side of the bus, and was about to roust Roc so I could go inside and grab another when he lifted his head. He rose and loped toward the wooded curve of the driveway whimpering, his tail making circles in the air. Since this was a behavior I'd not seen in all our years together, I rose to follow.

At the edge of the tree line, where my crushed-shell driveway opened into the clearing, a yellow bicycle appeared followed closely by a black one. By this time Rocco was going nuts with joy. Cassie dismounted, letting the yellow bike drop. She opened her arms to the big oaf who planted his paws on her shoulders and slobbered all over her face. Rita straddled the black bike, laughing. I stood twenty feet away, mouth hanging open.

"You're gonna swallow a fly, dude," Rita hollered through her laugh. Rolling past the gaudy display of affection, she stopped and flipped the kickstand down with her booted heel. She dismounted and joined me to watch Cassie and Roc.

"What's your dog's name?"

"Mud right now. Usually Rocco."

"He kinda likes her."

"Ya think?" I looked at Rita. "What are you two doing here?"

Still watching the disgusting display of mutual affection, she said, "I told her you were really fucked up and not getting your work done, and Rosie was gonna fire you."

"That's not true."

"The fucked up part is. I just added the rest to, you know, put a little drama into it."

I shook my head. "What'd she say?"

"She told me about the bullet hole; how she freaked."

"You already knew that."

"Not from her angle." She faced me. "Also, she told me why."

She had my full attention now. "Tell me."

She shook her head. "Do I look like a fucking reporter? I told her she had ta tell you, 'cause you were way too dumb to figure it out for yourself."

"I'm not sure I can live up to your high opinion of me, Rita."

She smirked. "Anyway, at coffee this morning I asked her if she was gonna tell you. She said she didn't know. Sooo ... I said we oughta take a bike ride and talk some more." She spread her arms wide taking in my clearing. "And here we are!"

When I looked back to the end of the driveway, Cassie was walking her yellow bike toward us, Rocco close by her side. The smile I'd so much wished for was absent, replaced by a worried frown. She set the kickstand and approached, stopping within arms length. Rocco sat next to her.

"How are you, Sarge?"

"Been better." I wanted so badly to reach for her that I had to jam my hands deep into my pockets and clench my fists to keep them there.

Cassie stroked Rocco's head and faced Rita. "Rita, come meet Rocco." Scratching the mutt's ear, she looked at him. "Sweetie, this is Rita. She's my friend."

 Rita stepped forward, reaching her hand out, palm up. He nuzzled it. She looked at me. "Does he like the water?"

"More than air," I said.

"C'mon Rocco." She jogged toward the Sound, her ridiculously heavy boots embossing the sand with the crosshatch pattern of the soles. Rocco hesitated, eyes on Cassie, taking off only after she nodded. I nodded too, but he was already gone.

"Want a beer?"

She shook her head. Walking past me, she pulled another chair from under the table and arranged it to face mine before she sat. I returned to my seat. She said, "I'm ... I'm sorry about ..."

"Cass?" I leaned forward, elbows on my knees, hands clasped. "Don't waste time on an apology. Just please, please tell me what the hell happened?"

She chewed her lower lip until I thought I'd see blood then began.

"I used to live in Montgomery, until two years ago. I was married to a professor at Auburn, a physics professor." She clasped both hands at the back of her neck, pressing her head against them before continuing. Her eyes were wet. "We were downtown one night, a warm night, walking from a benefit dinner at the Civil Rights Museum to our car. It was only a few blocks." She hugged herself, knuckles turning white. I wanted to reach out to her but I, even I, knew that was wrong. "We turned a corner and three young men ... they wanted money ... Lloyd reached for his wallet ... one of them ... so many shots ... like he was being punched each time by invisible fists ... so much blood." Tears streamed down her face and her eyes were focused inward, reliving the horror. I'd been to that place too many times. I knew what she was seeing. "When you told me you'd been shot ... it ... all flooded back at once ..."

Maybe it was the fact that I'd already consumed two brews; maybe it was because I was trying to get my head around things. Whatever the reason, my brain flipped into the analytical autopilot that had been so much a part of my past. "Did they catch the guys?" I heard my voice, flat, all business; and I couldn't help it. I was an Air Cop again.

She shook her head, frowning. "I ... I don't think they tried very hard." The pain in her eyes was heartbreaking, but there was anger in her voice when she added, "Lloyd was black."

About a hundred bells rang in my head, triggering terrible hidden memories: my old man's backwoods Tennessee bigotry, my mother's explanations that 'negroes were just less perfect children of God to be pitied not hated,' ... I buried my anger and asked, my voice steady and calm, "Was the shooter white or black?"

She looked worried as she answered. "White ... You sound strange."

I struggled to pull the retired Sarge back, to re-bury the old one. "How long did the cops work on the case?" I took her hands and held them, my breathing slow and measured, silent until I was sure he was present.

She shrugged. "I don't know. Not long. They said ... they couldn't locate ... that my description wasn't ... " She looked at me then. "I thought I had put it behind me ..."

"Cass ..." I knelt in front of her, kicking my chair out of the way. "I'm so sorry... Did they hurt you?"

She shook her head. "They screamed awful things, but no ... some other people heard the shots and ... yelled and ... they ran away."

"Cass, I can tell you from way too much experience with violence, you won't forget it - ever. Eventually you'll figure out how to keep it from taking over because you have to, to survive. It will always be there, but you'll learn to deal with it. Trust me, you will ... in time." She closed her eyes letting the tears flow. I kept holding her hands, waiting. After several minutes her eyes opened, her anger replaced by a profound sadness. With a quick squeeze she let go and leaned back in the chair wiping her eyes with the back of her hands. "May I have that beer now?"

"Coming up." I rose and hustled up the metal steps.

I returned with two cold longnecks, toed my fallen chair erect with a really slick move that was immediately negated when I tripped over the table leg. I landed on knees and elbows but managed to keep the beer from spilling. Cassie was laughing when I crawled over to hand her one.

"I'll give you an eight on that."

"I think I deserve at least a nine. The hook-toed chair lift is a particularly difficult move." I eased into my chair, brushing sand off my knees with my free hand. "I grant you the landing wasn't perfect."

She took a long swallow. Leaning forward in the chair, she frowned. "Sarge?"

"Mm?"

"I saw something in your face when I was telling you... something really strange ... almost, well ... it scared me a little."

I nodded. "Me, too."

"Would you like to tell me about it?"

I smiled. "Is that a psychologist talking?"

She shook her head. "It's somebody who's starting to care about you and wants to know you better."

"Just starting? I must be slipping."

She stood, glaring at me. "If you're in the mood to be a smartass, I'm leaving." She slammed her beer on the table and turned toward the bike.

"Cassie! Wait!" I grabbed her arm. "I'm sorry. It's ... it's old stuff that got pulled up by your story. It's really uncomfortable ... hard to talk about."

"You think what I just told you was easy?"

"No, no." I took a deep breath. "Come on back and sit."

"I will, if you'll tell me."

When we were back in our seats, I told her. I told her how I'd grown up dirt poor in the Tennessee back country, how my old man tried to get me to hate blacks the way he did, how all my friends were black share-croppers' kids, how I could never buy his shit about them, how my first sex was with a black girl a year older than me, how a week later the Klan hauled her into the woods and raped her, and how I found out my father was a Grand something in the Klan. By the time I finished I was stone sober, angry, and crying. I shook my head, trying to dislodge all the shit that was in it. I took a long ragged breath, then another, and finally felt my control returning.

Cassie nodded then sighed. "Where do we go from here?"

I shrugged. "I wish I knew." We sat sipping beer, lost in our own thoughts for several minutes before we made eye contact again.

Her face was relaxed with a hint of mischief in her eyes. "Where you like?" she said. I couldn't help it. I started laughing. Cassie joined me and our laughter got quickly out of control; tears in our eyes, we guffawed until we both fell out of our chairs, holding our sides. By the time we'd exhausted ourselves we were wrapped in each others' arms, sand sticking to our bodies.

Rita and Rocco, both soaked, ambled toward us; her boots were laced together and draped over the dog's back.

Cassie saw the two soggy playmates shortly after I did. She untangled herself from me and rose while I lay there admiring her graceful ... well graceful everything.

"You two look like you've had fun," she said. "Rita, go shower over there." She pointed to the outside rig. "And take Rocco with you." Remembering MY parental advice to the tattooed teen, I waited for Rita's verbal explosion. Instead she smiled and made a quick left toward the shower. As she walked away from us, she pulled the black tank top over her head. I was in the middle of a critical assessment of the artwork on her back when Cassie blocked my view. "Go get us some lunch at Island Convenience." She stepped closer and turned my head toward the Jeep. "That way."

By the time I got to my feet and shot a quick glance over my shoulder, Rita was through the shower door. Cassie slapped me on the butt. "I was just ... do the tattoos cover ..." I stammered by way of explanation.

She pointed to the Jjeep. "I need gas anyway," I said and hopped in.

Half an hour later I returned with three Carolina barbeque sandwiches and slaw. Rita was curled into my chair wearing one of my *Soundside* T-shirts, her maroon hair still damp. Cassie straddled Rocco, drying him with one of my large beach towels. I swear the mutt was smiling. The sound of my old washing machine chugging away caught my attention.

"I put Rita's things in the wash," Cassie said, answering my question before I asked it.

"It's not very efficient you know," I said, asserting my masculine practicality. "... using so much water for just a small load."

"Oh, it's a full load. I assumed that most of the clothing strewn around your bedroom had been worn several times, so I added that to the wash." Defeated, I passed out the sandwiches then dragged another chair over and sat, trying to look martyred but failing to hold back a grin.

Rita and Cassie chatted while we ate. I listened, marveling that women always seem to have something to talk about, always. During lulls at *Soundside* I do a little people watching and so often I see it – men sitting at a table chomping away, the only sound their chewing or an occasional grunt – while women spend as much time talking as eating, maybe more. Rocco lounged at Cassie's feet. I think he was making the same observation.

I was about half finished with my barbeque when the washing machine completed its final spin, so I scooted inside, stubbing my toe on the doorsill, and transferred the clothes to the dryer while I swore. It's amazing how a little profanity somehow makes pain more bearable. I could hear laughter as I approached the door. It stopped when I stepped out, leading me to the conclusion that I was the subject. Rita and Cassie were having more than a little trouble containing themselves but none at all staring at me while I descended the metal stairs.

"What?" That simple word caused an explosion of laughter that continued for several seconds while I stood with a goofy grin on my face, wondering what the hell was so funny. When things finally got quiet, I asked, "What the hell's so funny?" Which started them guffawing all over again. I gave up and sat.

Eventually they both quieted down. Cassie said, "I'm sorry, Sarge."

"I'll ask again, what's so funny?" They looked at each other. I braced for another episode of hysteria, but they seemed laughed out. "Well?"

"Nothing ... really," she said.

"Tell him, Cassie," Rita added.

"Yeah, tell him, Cassie." I was feeling a little grumpy.

"Well ... okay." They exchanged another quick glance. "We were comparing notes ... about how charmingly clumsy you are." She looked at Rita again, who nodded. "Did you really fill your pocket with water from a coffee urn?"

I glared at my smirking young co-worker. "I can explain that. A filled forty-five cup urn is heavy, so I was bracing it on my hip ... and the spout caught in my pocket." I waited while she giggled. "It only happened once." Rita put up two fingers. "The second one was coffee, not water, Rita." That brought on another short burst. "Okay, okay. I get it." I sat back, arms folded in a convincing sulk. They ignored me. While I was sulking and being ignored I observed that for the first time in the several months Rita and I had been acquainted, she seemed totally at ease. There was no hardness in her face, no wariness in her eyes, just a young woman relaxing with a friend. She must have sensed my attention because she turned her head. Her easy smile when we made eye contact told me she was relaxing with two friends.

I managed to bribe Rocco to join me by offering him the last bite of my sandwich. He inhaled it then sat drooling in front of me waiting for another one while I watched the ladies finish theirs. "Hey. How about we take a ride down to Canadian Hole?" I asked.

Cassie swallowed her last bite in one gulp. "Canadian what?"

"Canadian Hole," Rita answered before I could respond. "That's where the Canucks go to windsurf and shit like that."

"It's not only Canadians that go there," I countered.

"But mostly."

"Yeah, I guess that's true." It really didn't matter, I told my grumpy self. "Anyway, the kiteboarders and windsurfers down there are really pretty good." I stroked Rocco's head. "Wanna go?" They looked at each other, shrugged and simultaneously said, "Okay."

Rita explained more about the place, adding that Ego Beach on the ocean side was "really cool" when the wind was right. She kept up her monologue until the dryer buzzed, then she hurried up the steps and disappeared inside. A minute later she emerged in her black shorts and tank top, socks slung over her shoulder. She sat to add the socks and jump boots to her outfit, wrapping the long laces twice around just above her ankles. I had the odd urge to show her how to lace them air-cop style. Finally we all piled into the Jeep, Rita and Rocco in back, and headed south. Then we had to stop at Rita's and Cassie's, so they could "grab a few things" before we were actually on our way. I started wondering if we'd ever actually get there.

BJ Ross had her gear rental concession set up in a far corner of the parking lot. She lounged in her beach chair, shaded by a rainbow-hued umbrella; the back doors of the old UPS truck she'd painted with images of wind boards and kites, sat open. A young man carried one of her rigs toward the launch area. "Hi, hon!" she called when she saw my Jeep pull in. I parked a few slots away and hopped out. I turned just in time to be wrapped in BJ's arms. She was almost my height and still had that professional surfer's body even though she'd been unable to compete since blowing out her knee eight years ago. BJ gave the kind of full-body hug that made a guy want to stay that way forever. "It's been a while Sarge. Damn, it's good to see your raggy old carcass again." She whispered. After much too short a time, she stepped back to acknowledge my passengers. "I know Rocco..." the mutt wagged his tail at the sound of his name. "...but not your lady friends." She walked past me, aiming directly at Cassie with her outstretched hand. "I'm BJ."

"Cassie," Cass responded returning the handshake. "This is my friend, Rita." Rita nodded, eyes down, arm around Roc.

"You're quite a work of art, gal." She reached the Jeep and leaned down to let Rocco slobber all over her face. Rita smiled briefly. "You folks come to surf The Hole?"

I was about to say we'd just come to watch when Cassie and Rita answered, "Yes."

BJ got them set up, verified that Rita had experience as a windsurfer then turned to Cassie. "How about you, Hon?"

"I grew up in San Diego," Cassie said. "I was on a surfboard almost as soon as I could walk."

"Well that takes care of part of it, but yours didn't have a sail so let's go over some dos and don'ts." BJ's instructions were concise, her demos short and her advice simple, "Take it easy until you feel comfortable." Cassie nodded then she and Rita adjourned to the changing rooms. They emerged in bikinis, Cassie's dark green and Rita's, to my great surprise, white. Once they were successfully launched, BJ went back to her umbrella chair and I sat on the bumper of her truck. Rocco scooted under the truck for shade. I watched as Cassie familiarized herself with the rig, cautious at first then venturing a little more speed. Rita was performing all kinds of acrobatic maneuvers, a little too recklessly I thought.

"Your tattooed lady's pretty good." I nodded. "A little young for you isn't she?"

"I work with her."

She pointed to the north side of The Hole. "The other one's getting the hang of it." I looked over to see Cassie manage a short leap. "You got the hots for that one, Sarge?" I felt my face redden. "You have! Well I approve. She's a honey."

Both Rita and Cassie beached about the same time, dismasted their boards and dragged them up to BJ's truck, laughing and chattering. Rocco rose and loped out to meet them.

"You gals go change," BJ said, rising to meet them. "Sarge and I will put things away."

Ten minutes later we were headed north in the Jeep.

"BJ's nice," Cassie said then after a long pause added, "You two seemed pretty friendly."

"She's a friendly gal." I glanced at her and thought I saw what the next question would be, so in the name of full disclosure I volunteered, "We were a lot more friendly last year." The ensuing silence made me think that might have been too much information. "It was really nothing," I added, "Just a couple of ..." Rita leaned forward near my left ear and whispered, "Shut up, dummy." So I did.

When we neared Salvo, Cassie said, "Drop me at home." I was about to mention her bike but it seemed best if I said nothing. I pulled into the small parking lot and stopped in front of the staircase to her apartment. She hopped out, walked around the back of the Jeep, hugged Rita and Rocco then hurried up the stairs. Rita moved into the front seat.

"What did I do?"

"Women don't wanna know their guy's fucked another woman. Especially when they met them."

"But I didn't even know Cassie then." I shook my head.

"Don't matter. Look, let me off at my place. I'll talk to her over coffee tomorrow."

Driving home, I complained to Rocco that I'd never understand women if I lived to be a hundred. He slept through it.

That night, I sat outside trying to decide whether to head over to Paulie's or just have a few beers with Rocco, neither one with a chance of getting Cassie out of my head. I told myself I'd done just fine without her and I'd do just fine again – myself told me I was full of shit. I was on my way to a deep dive in the pity pool when my cell phone vibrated. I hauled it out of my pocket hoping it was Cassie, but Rosie's name lit up the screen. "Hey boss, what's up?"

"I need you to come over to my office."

The worry in his voice made me hurry. I hopped in the Jeep and hauled my butt over to *Soundside*. Rosie's office door was open. He sat behind his desk, hands flat on the desktop. "Close the door," he said. I did then sat in the only other chair in the small office.

"What's up, Rosie?"

"Rita's mom is in the hospital." That statement and his tone when he delivered it told me several things: Rita wasn't a runaway, Rita's mom was a friend, and Rosie was really scared.

"Have you told her?"

"I just heard a minute before I called you. Here's the thing." The big man hesitated then leaned forward, hands clasped tight. "It was Rita's old man who put her there." Rosie had my full attention now; I straightened in the chair. "Leanne, that's her mom, said he wanted to know where Rita was. She took a helluva beat down 'fore she told him. I'm going to Savannah tonight, to bring her back here." He inhaled long and deep before adding, "You take care of Rita while I'm gone."

"Why me?"

"The motherfucker will be headin' this way. We can't let him get to her."

"But why me? Why not just alert the sheriff?"

"Two reasons. One – She's still officially a minor – cops can't stop her old man from takin' her. Two - you were a cop. You can protect her."

I sat back in the chair. "Air Police, Rosie. I checked IDs, directed traffic, and escorted drunk officers to their quarters."

Rosie opened the folder on his desk. "There's a couple things make me question that." I watched him flip a few sheets then run his finger about half way down the page. "This looks all copasetic, you hoppin' place to place every couple years. Until ninety-six, when you get orders for a *special assignment*." He looked up, eyes narrowed, and closed the folder. Tapping it with a huge forefinger, he continued. "Says in here you was at the Pentagon, but there ain't any record of you livin' within a hundred miles of DC. There's no record of you livin' at all until oh-eight, when you show up at Lackland as the air police squadron first sergeant." At least now I knew how deep Rosie's PI buddy could dig.

"How's that make me a bodyguard?" I asked. "That *special assignment* was just a highly classified desk job."

"Don't bullshit me, Puppy. Nobody disappears to do a desk job." He picked up the folder and held it in both hands without opening it. "When you were in training you scored top of your class in damn near everything involving combat. Real soon after you went poof, some really bad folks in some really bad places started disappearing. That kept happenin' all the while you were gone."

I sat silent for a minute or more, Rosie's eyes locked on me, waiting, patient, knowing he had me. If I denied his claim I was pretty sure he could name names, names I never wanted to hear again. "What's her old man look like?" Rosie opened the right hand drawer of his desk and pulled out a photo. He handed it to me. It took a minute for me to recognize the heavy-browed man glaring back at me. "Isn't this Billy Joe Harman?" Rosie nodded. I stared at the face of the former Chicago Bears middle linebacker that sports writers had nicknamed *Hitman* after he'd put two running backs out of commission in consecutive weeks. I shook my head. "You're sure he's coming?"

"Cops between Savannah and here know there's an assault warrant out on him, but it'll be one of hundreds of warrants." Rosie clenched his massive fists. "We can't take the chance he'll be caught." He slammed both fists on the desk, causing a localized earthquake in the office. "I shoulda killed the mother when I had the chance."

"How much does he know about Rita out here?"

"For sure where she's stayin'; probably whatever her and Leanne talk about, you know, friends, work." That meant he could know about me ... and about Cassie! Rosie continued, "I'll call Rita now, tell her I'm goin' for her mom and to lay low till you get there."

My air-cop brain had been working on options while Rosie talked. "No," I said. "Tell her to pack some things and wait for me, and not to talk to anybody." I rose and held the photo out to him. "Can you get a dozen copies of this real quick?" He nodded and took it. I hauled my cell phone out and hurried outside. I tapped six on my speed dial.

"Hi Sarge. No contact for months and now twice in one day!"

"I need a huge favor, BJ."

"Name it, Hon."

I laid out the whole story for her, Leanne, Rita's dad, what I thought he knew about her friends, and ended with, "I need a place for Rita and Cassie to hole up for a couple of days."

After a short silence, BJ asked. "Wouldn't he know about me also?" I could hear the hint of fear in her voice.

"Rita didn't meet you until this afternoon. She never had the chance to tell her mom about The Hole."

"Okay. When you coming down?"

"Soon as I round them up. And thanks." I put the phone in my pocket and climbed into the Jeep. Rosie came out with copies of the mug shot.

"What you got planned?" he asked.

"Better you don't know, Rosie." He handed me the copies. I started the engine and headed for Rita's crib.

The terror in Rita's eyes was so palpable that I wondered how much more afraid I should be. She hurried to the Jeep as soon as I stopped, and threw her arms around my neck. I held her for a bit then took her shoulders and pulled her loose so I could see her face. "Rita, listen carefully. Run back up and tell your roommates you're going with Sarge. Then haul your butt back here. Hurry." She shrugged out of her pack, tossing it into the back then took the stairs two at a time. Seconds later she hopped into the front seat. "You have your phone?" She nodded. "Call Cassie. Tell her to pack." I spun the Jeep around on the narrow sandy lane, turned south on twelve and hit the gas hard. In the two minutes it took to get to Cassie's, Rita sat hugging her knees to her chest, sobbing.

I pulled into the parking lot just as Cassie reached the base of the stairs. Rita jumped out before the Jeep came to a full stop and ran into her arms. "We've gotta hurry," I called. Cassie pried Rita loose, picked up the bag she'd dropped and tossed it in back beside the pack. Rita hopped in after it, settling herself between the two pieces. Cassie climbed in front.

"Where are we going?" she asked.

"Buxton." I kicked up some sand on the way out of the lot and headed south. Cassie turned in her seat and leaned toward Rita, their heads almost touching before either spoke. I couldn't hear what they were saying over the wind noise in the open Jeep, but I didn't need to. Rita would be pouring her pain and fear out and Cassie would be listening, encouraging, consoling. I burrowed deep in my own head, trying to figure a way to avoid doing what I probably had to do.

The access road to BJ's property, nestled up against Buxton Woods, ended at her gate. I pressed the buzzer and watched the security camera focus on the Jeep for a second before the gate swung open. You don't make a ton of money as a professional surfer, unless you're a six-foot tall knock out gorgeous mongrel with a Hawaiian mother and Norwegian father, whose picture can sell a million surfboards, oceans of lotion, and bikinis that no other woman looked quite as good in. Her endorsements and smart investments set her up for life. The rental business was her way of socializing. Cassie's frown said volumes when BJ met us at the foot of the porch steps. BJ saw it too, because she came immediately up to Cassie, crooked her finger and when Cassie leaned close, whispered something in her ear that left her with a broad smile. I wished I knew what it was ... or maybe not. Anyway, Cassie hopped out and grabbed her bag. Rita started to follow then turned to me. "You sure he won't ... come here?"

BJ answered for me. "Sweetie, you and Rocco are buds, so you must be a dog person, right?" Rita nodded, puzzled. "Well meet Zeus and Apollo." She pointed toward the dark part of the porch where two huge mastiffs sat like statues. "They patrol the grounds at night. They see that you, Cassie, and I are friends ... and they know the bozo behind the wheel, so they're cool. But, if somebody who doesn't belong comes on the property, they'd face about four hundred pounds of hair, teeth, and eyeballs."

BJ reached a hand to help Rita out of the Jeep. "Okay guys, come meet our guests." I headed back up the driveway watching Cassie and Rita cooing over the beasts who could have towed my Jeep to Kansas if BJ told them to. I stopped worrying about them and turned to worrying about me.

I hit the speed dial for Rosie's cell. He answered on the second ring. "Everything okay, Sarge?" I could hear the anxiety in his voice.

"Rita's safe. Cassie's with her." He let out a sigh. "Where are you?"

"About halfway to Savannah."

"Question."

"Shoot."

"You think Billy Joe will be armed?"

"Not him. He's a skin-on-skin sadist. Likes to feel bones break under his hands."

"You sure?"

"Never seen him carry so much as a pocket knife. Seen him snap a guys arm like a twig though."

"Thanks for the comforting words."

"You got a plan? I figure you got maybe an hour before he hits the island."

"Yeah." I ended the call and concentrated on what I hoped WAS an actual plan. I figured Harman would go first to Rita's. When he heard she was with me, he'd try to find me. I wanted that to be in a public place. Twenty minutes hard driving got me to *Soundside*. I handed Mac a copy of the photo and waited while he gushed over Billy Joe's exploits on the football field. "If he shows up, tell him I should be at Paulie's." I left him in mid-gush and drove directly to Paulie's, who likewise gushed over Harman until I stopped him. "He'll come looking for me. I'll be out on the back deck."

"What the hell are you gonna do, Sarge?"

"Talk to him, but I doubt he'll listen. But I want our conversation to be public so make sure all your barflies are alerted."

Paulie's frown brought his two bushy eyebrows together into one giant black wooly-bear above his nose. "I don't want any trouble here."

"Neither do I." I leaned on the bar. "Give me five minutes after we make contact then call the sheriff. There's an assault warrant out on him from Savannah so they should hustle over." I figured with Harmon finding Rita's place, querying the kids about me, then going to *Soundside* to get the news I'd be here, I had about an hour. Normally that would be three beers. Today it meant club soda with lime while I watched the sun set over Pamlico Sound. I was finishing my second club soda and wondering if I'd misjudged the timing when the door opened behind me.

"Where's Rita?" I turned my chair around to face him.

"Who?"

He grabbed handfuls of my T-Shirt and hauled me to my feet. "Don't fuck with me little man. I want my daughter."

"Two things you should know: one - she doesn't want you and, two - you need to back off."

He twisted the T-shirt tighter. "Or what? You're gonna hurt me?" He snickered like he'd told himself a joke.

I smiled. "I'm gonna hurt you regardless, but if you back off I promise to make it quick." Having someone several inches shorter and fifty pounds lighter say they're about to do you harm tends to confuse an oaf who's used to snapping arms like twigs.

He lifted me off my feet by my shirt and threw me over the deck rail. Though not my first choice, it was the aggressive move I was waiting for, the excuse to defend myself. Then I heard, "You're as fuckin' dumb as your dog." And that changed the parameters.

Hitting a crushed shell parking lot from a height of five feet is painful regardless of how good one is at taking a fall. As I got to my feet, in the seconds before Billy Joe was within reach, the flaw in my plan became evident. Of course Rita's roommates knew where I lived and would have told him. He hurt Rocco!

I felt icy calm settle on me as I entered the zone that made time shift so that everything around me was in slow motion. I had all the time in the world to break Billy Joe's nose, a collarbone, and both knees. I was on his chest about to crush his windpipe when Cassie screamed "No!" I shook my head, not sure what I'd heard. I looked up to see her standing a few feet away, hands pressed against the sides of her head. Then I heard the sirens. Slowly I got to my feet and looked down at the whimpering lump on the ground.

"Rocco," I mumbled. She grabbed my arm and led me to BJ's BMW parked next to my Jeep. "Better take the Jeep. I'm bleeding. Her seats." She hauled the blanket out of the Jeep and draped the passenger's seat then pushed me in. We pulled onto the highway just as the Dare County Sheriff's car swung in.

Cassie slid the BMW a little on the turn into my driveway. In the headlights I saw Rocco lying beside the stairs. When I hopped out, the goofball wagged his tail. I hit the speed dial for Janine, the local vet, at her home while Cassie comforted Rocco. We met Janine at her office. After a quick examination, she determined that Rocco had a couple of cracked ribs. She taped him up and told me to keep him quiet for a week until they had a chance to knit. While she was helping Rocco up, my cell phone vibrated.

The sheriff's deputy who'd taken the call wanted me to come in and make a statement. "Got all kinds of witnesses say he attacked you, but Jesus, man you sure busted him up. He's in the emergency room at Nags Head getting reassembled. Can you be here sometime tomorrow?" I told him I'd show up around ten.

We made Rocco comfy in the back seat of the Beemer then Cassie got in behind the wheel. "Take me up to Paulie's so I can get my Jeep then I'll help you with Roc."

When I returned with the Jeep, Cassie was sitting on the steps, a beer in each hand. I took one and started to sit but she stood and motioned me inside, where I saw she'd set up a big bowl of water and some towels. She spun a chair around so I could straddle it. "Sit and take off the shirt." Once I'd done so she started working on my back, cleaning it with the warm water, occasionally using a fingernail to dislodge a wayward bit of shell. I finished my beer and started to go after another. She pushed me down. "Take mine." I did. When she finished washing my abraded back, she picked up a bottle of rubbing alcohol and a cotton ball. As she opened the bottle she asked, "How many other beautiful women are on your speed dial?"

"What do you mean?"

"Well I'm sure BJ is, and now Janine ..."

"Janine's Rocco's doctor."

"How many?"

Feeling a little frisky, I said, "How many am I allowed?" She poured alcohol on my back. Rocco barely stirred from his spot on the daybed when I screamed.

"Am I in there?" I pulled out my phone and put her in number three.

"Yep." She finished tending me with no further bouts of agony involved then put everything back where she'd found it, stroked Rocco's head and cooed to him then pulled up a chair facing me.

"Who are you?" I was about give her a witty response when she raised a hand. "Don't you dare try to pass this off. I saw you get thrown off that deck. You were on your feet a second after you hit, and you were ready for him. I ... I thought you were going to kill him!"

She scanned my face, her eyes damp, afraid. I swallowed hard. "Cassie, if you hadn't yelled when you did I would have. Thank you." I sighed. "I only intended to put him out of commission, to hurt him enough he wouldn't want to ever bother Rita again, wouldn't be able to. But ... when I thought he'd hurt Roc, I lost it." I shook my head. "That has never happened before. Never."

"How many befores were there?"

"What do you mean?" I asked, though I knew.

"God Dammit, Harlan Richards! I just saw you do something that terrified me, and now you imply you've done things like that before?" She slammed her hands on the table. "Against every fiber of my better judgment I'm falling in love with you, and I don't even know who you are!" Two tears rolled down her cheeks to settle at the corners of her upper lip. She remained still, all attention focused on me.

Details flooded my brain; eleven years; nine missions; a life I'd tried so hard to forget. "Who ... or what, I was, I've spent a long time putting behind me." I wanted to reach out and touch her tears, to taste them, to postpone the terrible journey I was about to take Cassie on, but I knew I couldn't. More for me than her, I decided to ease into it. "In ninety-two, I was assigned as a trainer for the Air Force Special Ops Force. Kind of an Air Force version of the Navy Seals." She didn't move, her focus so intense it made me edgy. "It's not well publicized, not like them." Seeing that she was just waiting for me to get around to it, I took a breath and dug into the real story. "I don't have to tell you there are evil people in this world; you've seen names and faces of some of them plastered all over the news. What you don't know is that the very worst of those evil people are never in the news. They fly under everyone's radar; it's what makes them effective." I drained Cassie's beer. She brought me another. "In ninety-six I was asked to join a group that officially didn't exist. We had only three things in common: no family, a strong sense of right and wrong, and superior combat skills. I met the others for the first time when we assembled to meet our bosses."

"Who were your bosses?"

I closed my eyes. I could see the small conference room, the five permanent members of the UN Security Council, ten of us, two from each country: five men, five women. I shook my head. "I can tell you they were internationally known and had the welfare of the entire planet as their goal." She frowned but didn't pursue it. "That was the only time they met with us. We were introduced to our handler, a woman named Glenda. All our assignments came from her." I took a swig of beer. "We worked in small groups, never more than three, sometimes alone. We were given names and details about a person, particularly their crimes. The mission, in Glenda's quaint terminology was always to neutralize them."

"So you killed them." Her voice was flat, toneless.

"Not always."

"How many did YOU kill?"

"Does it matter?"

"How many?"

I stood and paced the small room. "Four."

"On how many missions?"

"Nine." I was sweating. "Okay? Look I've told you everything you need to know."

Cassie rose and closed the gap between us. She brushed the sweat from my brow then held my head so I had to look in her eyes. "You've told ME, Sarge. But you haven't told YOU everything you need to know."

"What the fuck are you talking about?"

"You've never talked about what you did."

"What the hell you think I was just doing?" She led me back to my chair then moved hers so she sat close, knee-to-knee.

"Tell yourself about your first kill." She took my hands. "Do it for yourself, and for me."

I fought the urge to get up and walk away. No way did I want to go back; I'd left that life so many years ago; no way I'm going back. But then I heard my voice describing the high camp in the Himalayas, the slave trader whose hobby was tech climbing lofty peaks, the night he decided to venture out and fell into a chasm, his frozen body visible fifty feet below us the next morning. I heard me describe the Afghan warlord who'd been selling arms and secrets to Al-Qaida while claiming allegiance to his government, how his head exploded seconds after I squeezed the trigger three-quarters of a mile away, how I saw through my scope blood and brains spattered on his wife and daughter. Then I heard me talk about two assassins: the one who hanged herself from the railing in her Paris penthouse, and the other who lost her way in an underwater cave while scuba diving. Finally I heard me describe the others *neutralized* by my team. By the time I'd heard the last one, I heard me sobbing and realized I was on the floor in a fetal position. Cassie knelt by my head, cradling it while Rocco licked my face.

When I woke my head was on a pillow. Cassie sat on the daybed with Rocco's head in her lap. She was watching me. "You carry heavy baggage, Sarge." She rose, careful of disturbing Roc. "I'm going to return BJ's car. You have a statement to make in about an hour and a half."

I sat up. "I slept here all night?" She nodded. When I stood, my various stiff joints verified it. She kissed me then left. "I'll pick you up when I finish with the sheriff," I said. In half an hour I'd showered, fed Roc and helped him outside, and put on relatively clean clothes. The Dare County Sheriff's substation was right on twelve in Buxton so it was a short shot to BJ's. The three ladies and two monsters were waiting on the porch when I pulled up.

I caught the tip of my sandal on the edge of the door as I hopped out, ending up on hands and knees. Zeus and Apollo took that to mean a wrestling match was afoot so I was immediately pinned beneath two slobbering behemoths. I thought BJ let it go on far too long before calling them off. As I approached the steps, Rita leaped off the porch into my arms. "You really beat the shit outta my Dad?"

"Pretty much."

"The motherfucker deserved it."

I pulled her off, holding her by the shoulders. "You are a potty mouth." She stuck out her tongue then kissed my cheek and ran up the steps into the house.

I looked at Cassie. "You ready?" She nodded and followed Rita inside.

"Got yourself a keeper there, Hon." BJ said after they'd gone.

"I don't know, Doll. After what she saw?"

"You're good people, Hon. Good people sometimes gotta do bad things."

"But you don't know ..."

"Don't need to. She knows. Don't let her go, Sarge. You'll regret it."

Cassie and Rita said their goodbyes with hugs and promises to get together then carried their bags to the Jeep. I started it and headed toward the road. "Rita, how about calling Rosie?" She retrieved her phone and a few seconds later, was chatting with both Rosie and her mother. I drove north on twelve.

When I glanced at Cassie, she reached for my hand. "Where are we heading, Sarge?"

"Where you like?"

-END-

www.ingramcontent.com/pod-product-compliance
Lightning Source LLC
Chambersburg PA
CBHW030336020726
47493CB00004B/1296